TERENCE, MESPHISTO AND VISCERA EYES

CHRIS KELSO

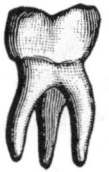

Bizarro Pulp Press
an imprint of JournalStone Publishing

Bizarro Pulp Press

an imprint of JournalStone Publishing
Detroit⤙San Fransisco
www.BIZARROPULPPRESS.com

Terence, Mephisto & Viscera Eyes
Copyright © 2014 Chris Kelso

ISBN-10: 0692240756
ISBN-13: 978-0692240755

Printed in the USA.

Cover Design: Jim Agpalza
Interior illustrations: Chris Kelso
Photography: Blair Dingwall

Interior layout by Lori Michelle
www.theauthorsalley.com

PRAISE FOR CHRIS KELSO

'Chris Kelso is a writer of almost intimidating intelligence, wit, and imagination. On every page there is evidence of a great mind at work. Just when you're wondering if there are actually still writers out there who still feel and live their ideas out on the page, I come across a writer like Kelso, and suddenly the future feels a lot more optimistic. One calls to mind Burroughs, and Trocchi's more verbose offerings— whilst remaining uniquely himself, in a writer as young as he is, is a very encouraging sign: one of maturity that belies his youth. I look forward to reading more from him in the near future.'

—Andrew Raymond Drennan, author of The Immaculate Heart

"Chris Kelso sets his photonic crystal gun on KILL and takes no prisoners. My favorite era of science fiction was the 60s "New Wave" when the British magazine NEW WORLDS took front and centre, and there's a bit of NEW WORLDS here, kind of like Jerry Cornelius using the cut-up method in a bungalow in Glasgow, with a splash of Warren Ellis added for extra flavour. Kelso has a compelling voice. Somewhere Papa Burroughs is smiling."

—L.L. Soares, author of LIFE RAGE and IN SICKNESS

'Chris Kelso is an important satirist, I think it's safe to say.'
—Anna Tambour, author of Crandolin

Someday soon people will be naming him as one of their own influences

—INTERZONE magazine

'Come into the dusty deserted publishing house where mummified editors sit over moth-eaten manuscripts of books that were never written . . . anyone who enjoys the work of my late friend William Burroughs will feel welcome here with Chris Kelso.'

—Graham Masterton

'Chris Kelso's prose swaggers like blues and jitters like bebop. Dig.'

—Nate Southard, author of Down and Just Like Hell.

OTHER WORKS BY CHRIS KELSO

Novellas
A Message from the Slave State
Moosejaw Frontier
Transmatic

Short story collections
Schadenfreude

Novels
The Dissolving Zinc Theatre
The Black Dog Eats the City

Anthologies
Caledonia Dreamin'—Strange Fiction of Scottish Descent (ed. With Hal Duncan)
Terror Scribes (ed. With Adam Lowe)
This is NOT an Anthology

CONTENTS

Come on and die
In your viscera eyes
Cataracts close the blinds . . .
—The Mars Volta

FAMILY MAN

THE GANGPLANK WAS covered in slaves, their rags swathed in sand and surf. The waves—a constant stirring of jagged V's boiled in hot foam—shook the vessel with all the mercilessness of the cosmos. Strange sunlight filled the top of the island with purple sand that glimmered across rows of elm and stretched the sage.

The Cherry Island marina was a clutter of ugly metal, scows in perpetual hither and thither, drifting landfills atop barges and freighters full of human cargo . . .

A child slave yelped and is punished just as the ship pulled into shore.

One slave, a woman—Amna—who was, one suspects, *born* into captivity, turned to her companion Gertrude and shared a terminal glance. When the slave masters were busy rounding up the men and bundling them into the water, Amna whispered into Gertrude's ear

—Do you know what they'll do to us?

Gertrude looked straight ahead at the wood-wreathed walls of their cabin, hopelessness her only permanent resident. She would not share another terminal glance with Amna.

A boy crawled around the deck, blood leaking from his anus. Slave masters stomped around him, kicked away any object the boy tried to grab onto to pull himself up. There was an ugly laughter, the kind only tormenters enjoy performing, and they were just that—tormentors. A meaty palm appeared and clutched the boy by the scruff of the neck. He pulled him to eye view. The meaty palmed man had a foul smirk, his words emitted in low-end murmurs of death breath that seized the nostril and spun the bag inside the belly.

—My own son—he repeated, again and again until the ugly laughter began once more.

TERENCE, MEPHISTO & VISCERA EYES

1.

—WAIT HERE DOG.

Phil latched Terence's leash to the railing and went into the store for cigarettes. Terence sat there patiently, waiting for his owner to come back out. There was a dull but bearable throbbing in his groin from his recent castration, like the rend and tear of a rusty saw on a numb, gangrenous limb. He sniffed the air around him. It was a good day to be a dog in Shell County—in spite of his new eunuchdom. The sun rode triumphantly in a curling mantle and he knew it would be Frisbee-throwing weather soon enough.

Terence often thought about his indentured servility and wondered how comfortable he really was about being someone's pet. No man or thing is born free, he supposed. A free man is dangerous, like a dog free of its leash. A free man is more likely to descend into entropy; the world around him would decline into chaos. A free man has no fear of God when he is his own god. *Any man (or dog) who has been purchased may eat if he has been circumcised.* The truth of the matter is that Terence had always been happy being a dog. It was all he'd ever known.

Phil came out of the store and primed up a cigarette. He huffed his first drag deeply, held the vapour in his lungs for as long as drawn breath would allow, before releasing a perfect cloud into the air and unhooking Terence from the rail. The sky became a tarp of plutonium orange.

—**Come on dog**—Phil instructed in a voice as deep as the Mariana Trench.

They walked through the park. Shell County didn't really have a 'park' for dog-walkers, just a mound of balding grass that led into a carnivorous woodland where local children went missing. Phil pulled at his cigarette morosely while Terence ogled the gambolling bitches and tried to remember that pre-op desire that once lingered in his loins.

They made towards a bench. Terence's owner was a depressing creature—a broken spirit trapped in an out-worn cage. His physical appearance suggested a raw deal of some kind. At 27 his hair had gone arsenic white; he was fat as a fool and his eyes were two limpid pools of insomniac anxiety—as if they'd actually penetrated the psycho-sphere and witnessed first-hand the coldness of the universe. He also smoked too much and hadn't had a job in over a year.

They say that over a period of time a dog will start to resemble its owner. Terence had indeed started noticing his own living decay. This was a concern.

***

The bitches ran pell-mell through the park's pathways. The air was perfumed with their thick scent, not that Terence harboured any carnal thoughts towards them, not since the humans severed him from the I-Ching. He took a shit on a well-flourished patch of grass and panted contently under the sun's blaze by Phil's side. He looked up at his owner. Phil was wearing an Irish sweater with cigarette burn-holes through it (from where he'd kept falling asleep watching TV with a half-smoked roll-up still smouldering away between his lips). He'd once been cool and mean; now he was just mean. Terence could see the change in his owner. Phil's life had taken a nosedive when his girlfriend Patty left him over a year ago. Terence never liked her much anyway. She flitted about the place like a hyperactive squirrel and never took the time to pet or walk Terence.

Another man appeared and sat next to Phil. He was overweight too and had a dark smudge around his mouth from where he'd been plucking Herod's worms from the soil all day long. When humans spoke, Terence only understood the occasional word, but his human-speak was getting better; more often than not their voices sounded like the rustle of barley fields or the echo of rills in a silent forest. He liked the noise of human-speak, as long they weren't shouting.

—So I guess you heard Patty got brutally raped while passing through Wire City?

—**Yeah I heard.**

—So, how do you feel about that?

—**Just another pervert with bad taste.**

Shell County was a sunken drogue that somehow sustained its own atmosphere. Everything that lived here was on its way out real soon . . .

—**How is the Stroboscope coming along? Anything we can put into practice yet?**

—Come on Phil, you know once the prototype is perfected I'll give you a cut of the action. Fuck, you're the most miserable guy I know—if anyone *needs* this machine it's you. Just be patient . . .

—**I dunno man, I'm at the precipice right now . . .**

—Don't be so dramatic. So Patty isn't coming back. At least you didn't have to deal with her *after* she'd been raped. Two victims in a relationship is the most self-destructive thing imaginable—that's one thing you don't need.

—**Okay, remind me again how the stroboscope works . . .**

—Eugh, again? Come on man . . .

—**Please? This is the only hope I got left . . .**

—It brings about a hypnogogic state, brings about a phenomenon of perception called Transmatica.

—**And it *can* help? You're sure it'll help me forget . . . even just for a few minutes?**

—It's just a lit cylinder with a rotating turntable inside . . .

—**Don't . . . don't do that, please. Don't devalue this thing, not this. You said it'll help; don't start back-tracking. Pulsing, rhythmic sounds to alter the frequency of my brainwaves or something, that's what you said . . .**

—I did say that, and I stick by what I said. When I hook you up to the 4D headset it'll produce a visual stimuli, geometric patterns right before your eyes, you'll be a slave to the eternal hum of the binaural beat. You'll forget—for sure you'll forget—just be patient till I figure out how to perfect my prototype . . .

—**Good . . .**

On the way home, Terence squinted at his own reflection in the storefront window. He was the same hot pink colour as Phil, had hair on his head just like Phil . . . the only difference was that he walked bowed on his feet *and* his hands. He noticed the smiling human-females reading their books and magazines on the knoll. Terence imagined that the people who wrote those books must be playboy millionaire geniuses.

—His prose is so crisp, so . . . what's the word? Crisp, yes. You almost forget you're a slave when you read his books.

—It's amazing, *uh*, just, *uh*, just amazing.

—How does he know what I'm thinking? He seems to *know* what I'm thinking!

—I know!

—How does he do it?

—I don't know!

—The way his words seem to effortlessly weave down the page and into my soul, into my fucking soul, *gah* . . .

It wasn't just the women either—men wearing spectacles were immersed cross-legged on the bench opposite. They tended to read quietly and with less audible enthusiasm, like a spider in tonic mobility. Instead they took in the writing as if their lives depended on its absorption. One bespectacled man across the path had his book open, clutched in one hand, as if he knew everyone was staring. As if everyone *knew* he was smart and deserved respect.

Since the castration, Terence could feel himself changing. He thought about his position as a dog, about his position as a slave. This new state of mind had granted him a strange clarity. Priorities were shifting. Terence wasn't satisfied with just chasing bitches all day long, he had to satisfy the hunger in his soul. He wanted to be respected; he'd never get it while some loser was dragging him around on a leash.

2.

THE CITY HUNG in a haze of its own black stink, like visions of Carcosa.

Terence wrote and wrote until his clumsy scrawling started resembling letters and sentences and his characters started resembling real people, not just a canine's caricature of a human being. All the while Phil recited the same mantra, going slowly insane with heartbreak and insomnia.

—*First she hit me, then she bit me, then she threw me in the truck and said 'you goin' wit' me!'*

Of course, by this stage Phil had completely neglected Terence. Losing Patty was something he couldn't get over and he didn't have the constitution to kill himself.

—**My feet stink and I don't love Jesus. What fuckin' hope have I got now? What a shitheel**— Before returning to his mantra—*First she hit me, then she bit me . . .*

Terence finished 10 stories altogether and kept them hidden under his dog bed. He was pretty happy with them and before long became convinced he'd be a landmark author of some kind. His grammar and spelling weren't perfect but he figured humans would appreciate the raw, authentic style—the fact he was a semi-literate dog would surely possess *some* novelty value!

He'd heard Phil having tantrums while trying to write letters to Patty, but hadn't been able to produce a single thing for months. Terence figured he'd somehow managed to tap into Phil's ailing creative spirit and steal all the good ideas from his head.

The only problem now was getting his work out THERE into the public sphere. He didn't know how the writing went from words on a sheet of A4 paper to a full-fledged and bound book.

Terence waited until Phil was asleep and started scouring the internet for an answer. Phil stayed in bed most days. He'd lost a lot of weight, stopped bathing too. Terence figured this was the new medication he'd become reliant on—apparently, junkies hate the feeling of water on their skin. Terence remembered Phil on the phone with someone earlier that day, which seemed to put him in an even worse funk.

—WHAT'D YOU MEAN THE STROBOSCOPE CAN'T BE DONE?? WHAT . . . I MEAN . . . YOU SAID . . . YOU *PROMISED* I'D BE FREE OF THIS NIGHTMARE!!!

Phil hadn't even noticed his newly literate, sexless Labrador plugging away on the computer, face lit up by the radiance from the monitor, the sporadic *click* *click* of the mouse under an eager paw. There was the castrato howl of stray cats outside—Terence's interest in them was minimal.

He eventually found what he was looking for . . .

TERENCE, MEPHISTO & VISCERA EYES

MEPHISTO—

Are you a struggling writer treading the line between manic depression and abject poverty? Mephisto Publishing has provided exemplary service to authors from all across the Slave State. Frustrated? Feeling emotionally raped by the industry? If you haven't been published, chances are people just don't 'get' you and the fat-cat publishing houses are too damn scared to put your work out there. Sick of the 'man' stepping all over you, preventing you from sharing your masterpiece? Mephisto has offered a platform for many writers who have experienced similar struggles. We are one of the original author-services companies and can offer you several different publishing options with traditional, full-service publishing to print on demand. What's the price of this great saviour? Absolutely nothing—just your dedication, best work, and a willingness to consolidate enterprises.

Receive your free publishing guide
After a meeting, you will receive your guide in eBook and e-mail attachment.

Reviewed manuscript
We will review your manuscript and pass it along to Mr Mephisto himself.

Full-service publisher
Our professional agents will edit, proof, create cover art, implement limited, defined promotional campaigns and take book orders from online

stores. Since consumption of books in digital
format is a rapidly growing distribution market,
Mephisto books are available in digital as well as
traditional print. The bottom line is, you are a
genius; we know it, you know it, now let's make the
sure the public knows it . . .

Terence hovered his paws over the keyboard tabs
and clicked on the e-mail address. He composed a
query letter and attached a document with his
favourite story, 'Human Digging up Bones in Soul'.

```
—Hello
I write stories. I just learned
speak. But I learn quickly. My
stories are good. You will like
them.
T
```

Terence clicked send. He felt confident and, sure
enough, a reply came zinging into the inbox minutes
later. If he still had a tail it would have been wagging,
his phantom erection stiff and true.

```
Dear T
We read your stories with
great enthusiasm and awe. As
divine agents acting from the
true will, we would like to meet
with you to discuss a publishing
strategy. Where can we meet?
Best
M
```

Terence yapped with joy. Getting published was

so easy! To think Phil moaned about being a writer, allowed it to ruin his relationships and bring about the onset of junky botulism. Terence didn't understand how *anyone* could fail at writing! Here he was, a Labrador with limited spelling ability, a near-certified published author! He was going to be the first dog writer. He typed up a message and arranged to meet at the park the next day.

3.

TERENCE SAT IN the park. A shadow etched towards him.

—Hello Mr Mephisto—he barked instinctively.

A voice emerged in response like a choir of demons.

—Mephisto is not one thing; I am just the civic intelligence, the face of Mephisto.

Its breath was of soil, damp and eternal, one with the alkaline earth—but the corpus was different. There was nothing organic about it. It seemed to've been cobbled together with old Pepsi cans and television sets stuck on a nebulous non-channel, filled between with some acrid heavy duty adhesive. It motioned forward in a slithering cube of gelatinous matter. Temporary eyes blinked open then disappeared beneath the body of the bubbling, shapeless amoeba-thing. Mistake of the elder gods . . .

—Well, hello all the same.

It bled fluid from every pore, viscera eked from the ducts—viscera eyes looked out at him with a cannibal's hunger. At least it seemed to understand Terence's inarticulate barking.

—You're Mephisto?—Terence asked.

—Mephisto is a network of individuals. Did you

know that the mind doesn't end within the prison of the skull?

—Um . . . no I didn't—Terence resisted the urge to clean his genitals.

—We act in concert to accomplish goals beyond individual agents to fulfil the hive wants, the propagation of information. In other words, the *ultimate* collaboration!

Terence wasn't convinced. He felt uneasy being out in the park without a leash on.

—Mephisto is aware of the dynamic evolution of knowledge between entities and eventually, through networking, we achieve distributed cognition.

—I don't . . . I'm just a dog . . .

—Mutualistic symbiosis, a knowledge ecosystem. We hope to increase the emergence of systematic acuity through stigmergy.

Terence squinted in confusion.

—You'll be connected by hyperlinks and your neurons and synapses will be replaced and amalgamated with the super-organism.

—I'm not sure this is what I was expecting . . .

—Things rarely are. You *will* get published, you *will* be part of something that commands respect. The leash is off.

—The leash is off?

—We just need to attach the vector—don't worry, it has no taste receptors so it won't enjoy the feeding process too much, we promise.

—That's good to know . . .

Mephisto materialised a tick-like creature engorged with blood.

—This will help transmit the virus into your system that leads to amalgamation.

He placed the wriggling arthropod onto the back of Terence's head. He felt it burrow deep into the fur behind his neck.

—But, what do you look like? I mean, the real you? The one up in the control centre; every organism has a navigator, or was that just human myth?

Mephisto sucked air into its maw, fluid bubbled in an exasperated throat.

—*It*, that is to say *I, Lem*, look more like a mole-rat. I'm rodent-like anyway, wrinkled skin. My eyelids are mere slits which suggests I have poor visual acuity when not assimilated with Mephisto.

This knowledge warmed Terence. It was good to know there was a simple animal up there just like him. He could really be part of something and succeed. He felt the vector bore through his flesh. This is the last time Terence would think for himself . . .

***

In the main nerve centre of Mephisto, both hemispheres discuss the latest readings of their newly amalgamated drone. They exchange dialogue via the colossus.

LEFT—His own brain is half the size of a human, which is remarkable given that a dog's brain is relatively tiny in comparison to that of a human being. The MRI suggest Terence has all the things we look for in Mephisto. He has intelligence, servility, and a desire for reward, but there's something else . . .

RIGHT—Okay, what is it . . .

LEFT—You might want to brace yourself.

RIGHT—Okay . . .

LEFT—It seems Terence has an exaggerated inferior, parietal region, advanced cerebral cortex, even a human-sized Broca's area, which explains his speech.

TERENCE, MEPHISTO & VISCERA EYES

RIGHT—So? He's a smart dog?

LEFT—No sir, I would say Terence is not a dog at all, but rather a human being.

RIGHT—Are you kidding?

LEFT—A human being with expressive aphasia. Don't get me wrong, he would be considered quite unfit to enter civilised society . . .

RIGHT—He looks like a dog to me.

LEFT—He tests positive for Pitt Syndrome, or 'wolfman syndrome'. He also has Rosacea which would give his nose that elongated, wet appearance. He is human in every other respect.

RIGHT—So, how did he end up as a dog?

LEFT—Memory mapping suggests he was in the care of one Philip Kohl; an unemployed slave, obsessive letter writer, and chicken hypnotist. He perhaps kidnapped Terence and raised him as a canine.

RIGHT—Good lord . . .

LEFT—We did an FMRI scan and he often dreams of being a human. Neurofeedback shows Terence strongly identifying with slave males. His castration may have helped him relate to slaves in his dreams. He's even started walking on two legs. You'd say he even looked like a human beneath it all.

RIGHT—We have to make sure he never finds this out. Break the last of his curiosity. Tell him his owner is dead. Take away his reason to ever leave Mephisto.

LEFT—But why don't we just unstick him? We can find another desperate writer to absorb, a human one.

RIGHT—You know as well as I do that separation after fusion is a long, complicated, humiliating process for Mephisto. You know what to do . . .

***

When news came out of Phil's demise, Terence couldn't help but whimper—which was odd, because what did Phil really ever *do* for Terence? Take him away from his home? Have him neutered? He had also showed companionship and love. Phil was a slave too; he was just waiting for his message to come through from the State consigning him to a life sentence mining inessential minerals in one of the enclaves. It wasn't Phil's fault he was a lousy owner.

—You hear the latest?—came a voice from the neighbouring cell. It was Lafitte. She was a rakishly thin girl with a blonde head of dirty, dry straw. Influences included Acker, Plath, and Anne Sexton. She too was an unpublished writer. Lafitte cradled a shrivelled baby in her arms that sucked her left breast into a dried-up bag.

—That Mephisto is really a communist composite committee called Stanislaw Lem, who was a parasitic extra-terrestrial life form who assimilated other organisms, an amorphous blob. It's back, self-replicating like a virus, a reservoir host . . .

Terence licked his own anus clean.

— . . . But that's just hearsay amongst residents who haven't received their full psychosurgery.

Her child, Persephone, had been born inside the Mephisto bowels—the first of a new jilted generation to be raised in its confines. She was a true phenomenon given that she had been *thought* into existence rather than conceived. Frankly, Terence thought it was cruel to breed inside this monster, even if it did encourage collaborative thinking. Lafitte often raved about how her child would be a genius, born within the super-organism. Persephone had been reared on information since the day of her birth.

That's why Lafitte claimed she took in so much of it; her drug starved baby would scream all through the night if it didn't get its second hand fix. There was some truth to this.

—No, what's the latest?—Terence asked, barely half-interested.

—They're synthesising a new strain of information, twice as hallucinogenic.

—Why would they do that?

—Apparently it'll encourage us to collaborate faster . . .

Terence didn't get too excited. Lafitte was far from a reliable source and her claims were usually erroneous. She specialised in speculative fiction.

—Who told you this?

—Raymond Hogg and I had a shared vision last night when we were on it. We saw the plan; we're crucial to the skein of the Mephisto organism.

Terence gave a suspicious look.

—It's true! Didn't you know that's how they communicate with us now?

—What?

—They blend the experience of two amalga-mates so they can have shared visions. It's the next big thing. Pretty soon all the public service announcements will happen through mutual transcendentalism.

—I haven't had any contact.

Persephone gargled, her inhuman eyes were pupil-less and milky, her throbbing brain engorged with culture.

—I was going to ask if you wanted to share an experience tonight . . . with me?

Terence became awkward. He really didn't want to share anything with anyone, especially a crazy cook like Lafitte. Being sexless was anti-social that way. He was, however, touched by her sentiment and he'd have been lying if he said he didn't enjoy the feeling of being wanted again.

—Maybe.

It seemed so easy for Terence to become amalgamated with the Mephisto body, leave his human owner Phil and finally get his work published. It soon became apparent, however, that it was something else. Optimists believe Mephisto's ultimate motivation was to wage guerrilla warfare on the cultural industry, run unorthodox solidarity campaigns for victims of the Slave State's censorship policies, repression and, above all, play out elaborate media pranks as a form of art. Terence felt like he was comfortable with what these people said Mephisto represented, at least he was a published writer now . . .

Viscera eyes bled into his mind, burrowed deep through the back of the skull, through bone tissue and matter until they reached the cosy caves of Terence's sockets. The vector outline rested under his skin, giving him a second pulse. Everything Terence said and thought was being recorded by the Mephisto CCTV set up behind his own eyes. He'd been tampered with so much that he just couldn't trust his own body anymore. They'd even fitted his collar with a bizarre device called The Bowlingual—a microphone transmitter with voice-print analysis that translated his barks. Terence grew accustomed to being awoken in the middle of the night and forced to undergo mutilating surgeries. He even thought that, perhaps, he was happier because of all the tampering.

But he knew, deep down he knew, that the huge lumbering monster he'd been absorbed into wasn't to be trusted. It wanted him to implicitly adhere to *its* ideologies and sacrifice the creative part of himself. He wasn't writing for himself anymore, reflecting his own inner desires or satisfying his own soul. He was a lobotomised lackey, an intellectual invalid working for a group who share their work. Mephisto was used by hundreds of artists and activists all over the Slave State and the Americas since the first failed emancipation, but the truth was that it was the monster who was using the artists. The Mephisto was more akin to a parasite that pulled in aspiring and naïve young artists to help feed its own ambition of world domination. Soon it spread to other Slave towns and cities, such as Wire and Ersatz, as well as countries outside the Slave-zone such as Austria-Germany, New Catalonia, and Soviet-Asia.

Terence's ears had seized up into grotesque fleshy muffs. This wasn't uncommon in the warrens. He observed Lafitte's haggard appearance, her emaciated, stretched face, saw her cross-eyed vacant stare—and felt nothing but pity, testament to the intrinsic goodness of a life that never received much in the way of sympathy itself.

It occurred to Terence that he could still end this pattern of servility. The truth of the matter was that he was exhausted. The life of a writer had run its course, like how a jaded cop must feel when he's seen one too many dead kids. All the awards that Mephisto won or was nominated for weren't enough. Mephisto wasn't enough. He crawled to the dark corner of the warren and lay there, the way a sick dog does when it's ready to die alone.

There was the initial rush of hypertension, then the crashing of the sea, and then came the blitzkrieg of colours . . .

Lafitte watched on as her child kept sucking until it finally released its teeth from the punctured, lolled balloon of her left breast. Viscera eyes stare out from her hollow sockets as Persephone dies in Lafitte's arms, face opaque as a film of creosote on the river. She died just in time, having drained her mother completely . . .

Philip K. Dick to the Slave State

(Attached for the interest of Slave State authorities, namely Baroness Un and her enabler Moog, is an intercepted, uncensored letter from subversive aggressor Philip K. Dick to the FBI on September 2, 1974)

—I am enclosing the letterhead of Professor Darko Suvin to go with information and enclosures which I have sent you previously. This is the first contact I have had with Professor Suvin. Listed with him are three Marxists whom I sent you information about before, based on personal dealings with them: Peter Fitting, Fredric Jameson, and Franz Rottensteiner—who is Mephisto's official Western agent. The text of the letter indicates the extensive influence of this publication, SCIENCE-FICTION STUDIES.

What is involved here is not that these persons are Marxists per se or even that Fitting, Rottensteiner, and Suvin are foreigners but that all of them without exception represent dedicated outlets in a chain of command from Stanislaw Lem in Krakow, Poland, himself a total Party functionary (I know this from his published writing and personal letters to me and to other people). I will refer to him as Mephisto for the remainder of this letter. For an Iron Curtain

TERENCE, MEPHISTO & VISCERA EYES

Party group dedicated to State suppression and manipulation purposes, Mephisto is probably a composite committee rather than an individual, since he writes in several styles—and sometimes reads foreign (to him) languages and sometimes does not—to gain monopolistic positions of power from which they can control opinion through criticism and pedagogic essays is a threat to our whole field of science-fiction and its free exchange of views and ideas. Peter Fitting has, in addition, begun to review books for the magazines Locus and Galaxy. The Party operates a [U.S.] publishing house which publishes a great deal of Party-controlled science-fiction. And in earlier material which I sent to you, I indicated their evident penetration of the crucial publications of our professional organization SCIENCE-FICTION WRITERS OF AMERICA.

Their main successes would appear to be in the fields of academic articles, book reviews, and possibly through our organization the control in the future of the awarding of honours and titles. I think, though, at this time, that their campaign to establish Mephisto as a major novelist and critic is losing ground; it has begun to encounter serious opposition: Mephisto's creative abilities now appear to have been overrated and it's crude, insulting, and downright ignorant attacks on American science-fiction and American science-fiction writers went too far too fast and alienated everyone but the Party faithful (I am one of those highly alienated).

It is a grim development for our field and its hopes to find much of our criticism and academic theses and publications completely controlled by a faceless group in Krakow, Poland (which incidentally is a city twinned with one Shell County, located roughly 500 galactic miles away in the 4th dimension). What can be done, though, I do not know.

END

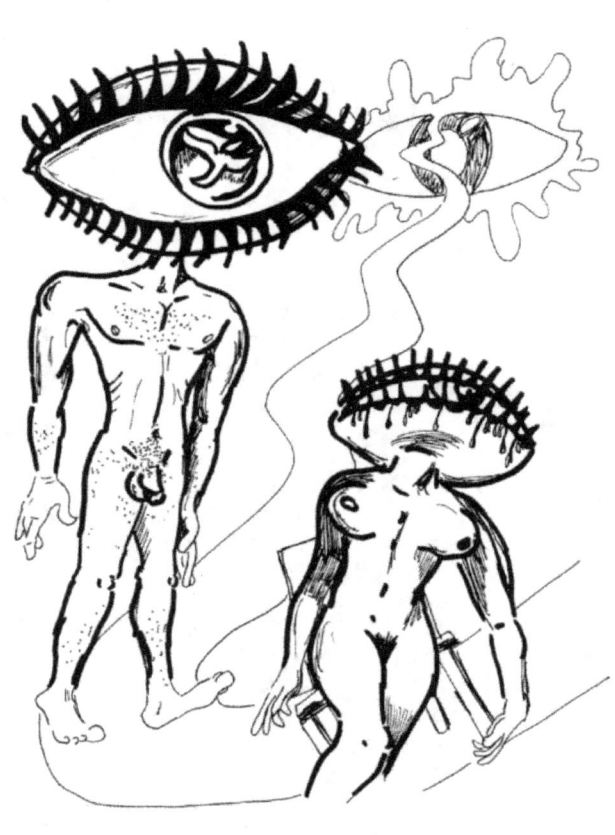

THE STATEMENT OF
TOM TRYOUT

1.

THE BIRDS WOULD watch Tom eat. They'd gather on the pier and leer at him, white as almond blossoms, as if they *knew* something.

Outside—a staccato of fireworks

Tom Tryout observed the wound he'd made in his girlfriend's belly. Its ripe rawness was almost vaginal, gaped to maximum resistance, leaking, budding ever outwards in ugly red shrooms of tissue.

Tom took out a syringe and dug it into the bar of Suzie's semi-rigoured forearm. He descended the plunger then brought it back up slowly. He brought it up to view, studied the measure of blood that filled the gauge. The Gangles outside squawked. He smiled. Tom could hear Mr Kowalski outside trimming his lawn with that old busted-up mower of his, the one with the stiff pull-chain and shifting mechanical guts as loud as an ironmonger's clank.

—I sure know how to pick 'em huh?—Tom addressed no one.

He rolled up his shirt sleeve and pinched the flesh on his bicep until it became rouged with the colour of sudden circulation. Tom stuck himself with the needle, sinking the plunger till Suzie's blood mixed with his within the great sarcophagus of flesh. Tom had an erection too.

—*No point ignoring it*—he thought out loud, unbuckling himself and seizing his thickened shank with a firm, murderous hand. He leaned over his girlfriend's detonated corpse and . . .

Tom looked down at his wilting penis and knew he just couldn't do it. He hated Suzie and everything she'd done to him, but raping her corpse seemed . . . a touch excessive maybe? They had only slept together once before. It meant a lot to Tom but not a lot to Suzie, and wasn't that always just the way with boys like Tom?

He was seventeen years old now. Suzie was his third girlfriend but the first one he loved enough to murder.

Cue soporific vibrations of a migraine . . .

***

Two Tuesday's ago . . .

It was trash day. Lines of refuse bins sat curbside, pregnant with garbage. Tom liked his seaside town. Every lawn on Shaver Point was lush and always freshly-cut for summer. Each house on his avenue sat prettily opposite the verdant greens with their panels of white timber.

He'd known most of his neighbours since he was a young kid, and liked most of them too. He thought they were all real friendly folks. Outside his window were the sounds of the brawling sea by the pier, the gentle idling of boats, of happy people, inner calm, arsenic white sands on the horizon like a sudden stroke of snow on coloured canvas . . .

Equally, there was much Tom *didn't* like about his street, mostly to do with *her* . . .

THE STATEMENT OF TOM TRYOUT

Love had left him with a great heaving anvil in his chest. He still hadn't gotten used to life without Suzie. He sincerely believed he never would, Tom being a teenager of suicidal ideation as it was.

Suzie lived three blocks from his house and he had to walk past her window on his way to school every morning. The pain was unbearable, cruel even. Tom felt sure he was being punished for something, maybe for giving his heart away too easily. He proceeded to move through life like a dismal flame, lath thin.

Tom couldn't help but look in the window as he walked past, squint through his own reflection. One time he was met with the hostile golem-mask of Suzie's father, who'd always hated Tom for being a wimpy sort of kid.

Suzie had just dumped him before spring break; it was all very sudden. She was going off to university to become a marine biologist or something. He'd never see her again, he was sure of it. Worse than that, Tom had been plagued by these crippling headaches since her departure. He figured it was just another one of those weird physical reactions to unexpected loss—he supposed his body was lacking the essential nutrients of love. Granted, Suzie was a beautiful girl and Tom really believed she felt the same way about him as he did about her.

Suzie said she still wanted to be friends, that they'd just drifted apart lately, no big deal—but Tom soon discovered the truth. Barely a week later she started dating Leo Kricfalusi. Leo tormented Tom growing up, now he'd stolen his girl.

It just wasn't fair.

***

The Winged Shaver Gangles gathered in a

suspended configuration—the white cartel. Tom's presence always seemed to induce an angry reaction from the birds. Upon mere sight of the boy the birds started weaving in a regimented formation, as if poised for attack, as if they saw his presence in the town as a threat. They'd squawk and jibe him in a chorus of rasping klaxons, they'd dive-bomb from the air and charge him beak-first until he was well out of sight, away from the pier . . .

Sometimes Tom thought they sounded almost human—WIMP, HEY WIMP! WIMP! WIMP! HEY, FUCKIN' WIMPY KID! Or—HEY, HEY PEANUT DICK? HEY, FUCKIN' PEANUT?

That awful, elongated screech. It was unreasonable.

The Gangles owned the pier. It seemed as if every Gangle in the world came there between migrations. A cull was out of the question; the town was named Shaver Point after all, and they couldn't very well obliterate the thing that made their town unique. People just accepted that they were here to stay and learned to accept them.

This one Gangle sat perched on a lamp-post a few blocks down the street from Tom's house, its talons cut in keen edges. He got out his telescope and mounted it on a tripod. This bird looked different. Tom stared until he met its gaze. Its eyes were like black buttons, impenetrable, fierce as the fiend in hell. He was certain the Gangle had a severed arm dangling from its yellow neb.

Eventually the bird soared off towards the pier with barely a beat of its wings.

***

On his way to the store for his father, Tom saw

THE STATEMENT OF TOM TRYOUT

Mr Kowalski mowing his lawn. He smiled at Tom when he walked past.

—Morning Mr Kowalski.

—Mornin' Tom m'boy! Powerful weather we're havin' huh? Looks like it's gonna be a good one! Damn Gangles aside . . .

—Yeah, they're acting weirder by the day.

—They're getting fat as fools!

—My dad had to put tension wire on the roof to stop them pulling off the insulation. Mr Kowalski tutted out loud.

—The celestial bird my keister!

Tom noticed the busted-up push mower the old man was using.

—You know, my dad has a cordless power mower if you need it?

Mr Kowalski gave a big jolly laugh.

—No, no. I'm okay with this ol' heap oh junk, don't you worry bout that. Say, you on your way to the store sonny?

Tom nodded.

—Here, pick me up a bottle of aspirin would ya?

Mr Kowalski tossed Tom three coins, not nearly enough for a bottle of aspirin.

—Sure thing.

—You're a good boy Tommy.

Tom hated being called Tommy but didn't mind it so much when Mr Kowalski said it. He was a harmless old coot. He was an old city guy from some grease-trap on the outskirts of paradise. You could really tell that Shaver Point brought him a lot of spiritual calm.

In the store, Tom picked up the aspirin along with a bag of pretzels and a blueberry slushy. His dad wanted him to pick up some fruit and milk, which he forgot to do. His skull was still throbbing a little so he took a couple of aspirin from the bottle he'd bought for Mr Kowalski and crunched them—his face twisted by the awful taste of flavourless medical powder. He caught his reflection in the convex mirror. He saw the horror of freedom and responsibility. For a moment he was grateful for his burden of agony.

On his way out into the parking lot he saw Suzie with Leo Kricfalusi. Something in his gut anchored. Tom tried to duck behind a parked Chevy but he'd already been spotted. He tried to remain cool, composed, his emotions kept in check.

Leo was an overdeveloped teenager with a quarterback's upper body strength and hurdler's calves. Leo was a stark contrast to Tom, who'd looked the same since he was twelve years old and would surely remain thin as a gold leaf until his senior years. Kricfalusi smirked.

—Hey Tommy, you out shoppin' for your mommy?

Suzie nudged Leo in the arm. She didn't like to see Tom ridiculed. She'd put him through enough.

—They're for Mr Kowalski—Tom countered lamely.

—Aww, look at you, always the Good Samaritan huh?

Tom put his head down and tried to brush past Kricfalusi but got body-checked instead. Tom's slushy tipped all over his shirt. Kricfalusi found this hilarious. He picked up the aspirin and threw back a few pills before tossing the bottle back at Tom. When Tom looked up, he was more hurt to see a cruel grin on Suzie's face.

Then, at the apex of his humiliation, something

wet and slimy cracked over his head and dripped down his face in foul streaks. Tom looked up and saw the Gangles circling. There was a maddened shriek and, on cue, a deluge of shit showered over the boy. They seemed ready to barnstorm. Tom wanted to just disappear, to not be standing there in front of Suzie covered in Shaver Gangle excrement.

After dropping off the aspirin at Mr Kowalski's place, and apologising for the half empty bottle, Tom ran straight upstairs to his room. When his father asked where the groceries were, Tom didn't reply. Dad was cool that way though, he always cut his boy some slack—after all, he knew what it felt like to lose your first love.

***

The following Tuesday, Tom was taking out two sacks of garbage just as the trucks were doing their rounds. He still hurt from his run-in with Suzie and Leo the week before; the whole ugly mess would be a long time in healing. Tom stuffed both bags into the container and was about to go back inside, when he stopped suddenly. One of the dump trucks was crushing up trash in its rear loader. The pneumatic grapple clutched another heap of bags and dropped them into the compactor. Tom watched on, mesmerised. His mind was fixed on fantasies about getting Leo back for all he'd ever done to him.

It would be tragic if he were to meet such an awful end. Then he could be with Suzie again. The soft murmurs of a migraine stole back his attention and he headed back inside with his hand clutched over his forehead.

This was the worst summer ever. Unlike Suzie, Tom hadn't bothered applying for university; he wanted to spend the summer with her before making any decisions about his future. All he knew was that he wanted Suzie to be in it.

The paintwork on Josie's house had been corroded by Gangle shit. Her parents were never home so it never got cleaned. If she hadn't been Tom's best friend he wouldn't have been seen dead going near that place.

Do you know about Hell's Orchard?—Josie asked, knowing the answer, knowing full well that Tom had articulated his fear about ever visiting the place. Josie often did that when she wanted to talk about something delicate but wasn't brave enough to just come out and say it. They made good platonic companions; Josie was stuck in the heart of her own existential nightmare.

—Course I know it.

—You heard about all those murders too then?

—I dunno . . .

—So why don't we, like, go down and check it out or somethin'?

—I don't want to, we have our last exam tomorrow.

—So? It'll only take, like, a sec . . .

The truth of the matter was that Tom had always been much too nervous to ever go near Hell's Orchard on the edge of town. It smelled of bygone nightmares.

—The rumours about him being a lizard isn't true . . . like, I'm sure of it.

—That's hardly my main concern!

The owner, *Mr Hell*, was a crapulous old man who shot dogs and stole children. Even Tom didn't want to cross the path of such inherent nastiness and evil. Josie dragged her nails through her long black tresses and flicked away the fringe with one jut of her neck. Josie's eyes were scored with gothic make-up. She looked at him past the fallen mask of hair and she grinned. Tom knew that grin. It meant she thought he was a chicken shit.

—I hear he can't kill women anyway because his reptilian Teiidae superiors are all female. Killing women is, like, totally against their culture.

—Lucky you . . .

—You still hung up on Suzie?

—A little . . .

—Hey man, like, fuck her. You can do better?

—You really think so?

—Well . . . nah, but, yano, I'm here for you n' stuff.

Tom heard the Gangles howling under the blister-bright sun, mocking him. Just like Leo Kricfalusi. While Josie was talking, he decided he would kill Suzie. It was the only thing he could think of doing that would alleviate this awful funk. His headaches wouldn't cease until he took action, until he stuck up for himself. Maybe then the birds would leave him alone too . . .

2.

MR ALHAZRED SCREAMED at his class to be quiet—his students fell dead silent. They hadn't seen him enter the room. Normally the kids in his classes shut their mouths just from the sound of his formal shoes clip-clopping down the corridor. This time they'd gotten sloppy; he caught them red-handed. When Mr Alhazred yelled, he yelled with his entire being. His jaw dislocated to a huge cavernous hole, teardrops of saliva shooting forth over the whole class.

—EXAM TIME YOU LITTLE PUKES! EXAM TIME, THAT MEANS SHUT YOUR GODDAMN SWILL HOLES!

Josie and Tom hadn't actually been misbehaving but took Alhazred's warning with a personal seriousness. He was wearing a summery T-shirt and Tom saw the Gangle in him—an ivory plumage with a dark mantle. Then there was that voice, that shrill, flustered screech which vibrated through your body like rickety train tracks beneath a hurtling locomotive. He reduced bullies to tears, irrevocably shattered the spirits of the sensitive. The only noise more ear-piercing came from the insane seagulls perched on the railings outside. Alhazred was a monster. They say he was possessed by the devil; it must've been something worse. It wasn't so hard to believe . . .

The exam hall smelled of teenage fear, the bubbling bile of anxiety . . .

Tom wasn't worried about his exams. He studied thoroughly and mathematics always came sort of naturally to him—in any case, extinguishing his ex-girlfriend the night before had left him oddly settled and focused. Even when a horde of Suzie's gal pals appeared in the corridor mumbling speculatively about her whereabouts, Tom wasn't worried. Even when everyone lined up in preparation to enter the exam hall and he could feel Leo Kricfalusi's stare follow after him . . .

He wasn't worried.

Worst case scenario, he'd kill them too.

—*Let them natter amongst themselves*—Tom thought to himself and remembered that—*the problem with women like them is that their cities have never been bombed and their mothers never told them to shut up.*

It was Bukowski who said that.

The invigilator, a stooping, bearded ignoramus, gave each student a number eight pencil and told them to begin. Tom opened his paper and started writing down answers to equations without really having to think. Ten minutes in, the invigilator started going into a semi-orgasmic sneezing fit.

—AHH . . . AHHH . . . AHHH . . . Jesus, it's comin' . . .

Tom, who was in the front row, directly under his gaze (and firing line), did well to ignore the haze of snot and sputum swarming from the invigilator's flaring orifices.

—It's com . . . AAAHHH-CHOO!!! CHOO!!! . . . eugh . . .

Tom finished his paper with plenty of time to spare. He turned it over and diligently folded his arms. The invigilator looked at him untrustingly; everyone else was writing or had their head in their hands. Tom used this time to re-live the more pleasant aspects of his relationship with Suzie.

. . . how her lips traced his mouth when they kissed

. . . like the way jagged objects whisper through layers of human flesh with devastating efficiency.

He could not contain a smile—a feeling that tunnelled through his molten core like a close range shotgun shell. Tom was an artist making figuration libre, a neo-expressionist maverick, too ahead of his time and all that . . .

—Here it comes . . . again . . . AAAAHHHHHH . . .

Tom fantasised about climaxing into Suzie's open stomach wound, watching in woozy satisfaction as the teardrop of fluid disappeared into the subterraneous chasm of webbed connective tissue, into the pits of her fucking soul . . .

—CHOOO!!! Oh, eugh, jeez . . . eugh . . . oh Jesus . . .

He could feel her blood in his body, snaking foreign arteries, mixing well with the host. Suzie would always be a part of him now, the thought of which freshly stirred his arousal; the anticipation of getting home to his own room to masturbate made Tom's belly ache. His brain swam in a reservoir of endorphins, his stiff cock under his desk begging to be strangulated. Tom started sweating.

The ache in his bowel grew more intense. His sphincter winked and puckered. Both testicles tightened up, his toes flexed. Tom wondered if he might cum without having to lay a finger on himself.

THE STATEMENT OF TOM TRYOUT

He decided to use Suzie's corpse that night. He wanted to lose his virginity to her. She was currently lying under his bed. *Her body won't have decayed too severely*—he hoped. Tom worried for a moment that her vagina might have seized up and become impenetrable. He felt it only once while Suzie was alive. Tom had never enjoyed sex.

The invigilator sneezed again and a bead of blood dribbled from his left nostril to the hairy camber of his top lip. His eyes spooled to the back of his skull until he was staggering around with the milky white eyes of a man possessed. He went to sneeze again but the pull-back was so prolonged you got the feeling that when he did eventually go to release, his entire internal organs would shoot from of his nostrils. He released.

(His entire internal organs shoot from his nostrils)

Everyone started screaming . . .

***

The Smiths were always on. He loved The Smiths; he and Suzie used to listen to them together all the time. He listened to "There is a Light that Never goes Out" and dragged Suzie's mannequin out from under the bed. Tom's room was a mess. He lay her supine in the middle of the floor and knelt at her feet. Tom was nervous, the ready-stiffness from the exam theatre long gone.

—This is it . . . *destiny*.

Her skin wasn't as hard as it looked; she had maintained a kind of rubbery smoothness. Tom decided he had to just bite the bullet, get it over with. He couldn't go through high school another day a virgin. He wrestled his trousers to just below his hips and yanked Suzie's skirt and underwear to her ankles. *That intrepid first step.* There was a strange smell, but Tom chose to ignore it for now. He lowered himself down on to her, gently bringing his lips to hers. Tom kept his eyes on her face—that pale, shocked mask with a mouthful of pause. Tom ran his trembling hands over her parchment-thin flesh, praying it might spark his arousal. Her delicate features, once flushed with sunburn, were now blued and chisel cold. He dreamt of making Suzie live again. The song ends.

He put his flaccid penis into the bloody trench of her stomach. He thrust in and out of the wound, each dip revealing a cock-end swathed in wet gore. Suddenly he felt a presence in the doorway—it was Josie.

—Tom, what're you doing?

Tom tried to maintain his composure and avoid scrambling to his feet ashamedly. He stood up, in his own time, in full frontal profile before Josie. Her eyes went to his flaccid penis. Tom could still feel the warm, wet heat on his cock, blood *still* soft as liquid velvet.

Maybe if he'd been more forthcoming when Suzie was alive she might not have left him. If he'd just *stuck it in her* the way Kricfalusi probably did. He couldn't help but think like this even though it achieved nothing. His head throbbed a little.

Josie looked back up at Tom's face and said— What'd you think of the exam then?

—Fuck, Josie, I . . .

—A demon of the first kind, eh? Relax, I won't tell anyone you fuck dead bodies.

—Really?

Josie shrugged.

—So, how many have you killed?

Tom's face fell to shock, he was instantly offended.

—How can you even ask me that?

—Have you eaten any part of her yet?

Tom bowed his head, nodded.

—Just one of her organs, the liver I think. I can't really remember.

—Huh! Well there ya go . . .

—And I think I tried some of her blood. I've been injecting myself with her blood, only because I loved her, you gotta believe me.

They both stood in silence for a few seconds, allowing the intensity of the situation to dim a little.

—What are you thinking Josie? Are you going to call the cops or . . . ?

—Heck, I'm just thinking, like . . . yano when you think you really know someone, like, they seem so predictable?

—I guess. I just wanted her to be part of me. When I was eating her, I don't know, it felt like something more intimate than sex . . .

—You should really try getting laid man . . .

—Please don't tell anyone, you can't tell anyone. Leo will kill me!

—Sure, all you have to is, like, something for me . . .

Tom's testicles crawled. He knew what Josie wanted him to do.

3.

HELL'S FARMHOUSE WAS like something from a horror movie. The crutch of a deformed sycamore split into twisted boughs of shrunken heads that dangled just above the roof. Tom and Josie saw the grid of mown grass and bare soil of the plantations that promised to hide all manner of atrocious nightmares from clear sight. Josie picked up a shrag from the ground and started bending it nervously.

—We don't have to do this—Tom reassured her.

—I *want* to do this. Stop being such a baby . . .

A sudden silver varnished the trees, the moon was out. The Gangles were silent but still present. Tom felt the wrought iron railing that led to the woodlet. He was cold, his head still felt ready to burst.

—Why do you want to come down here again?

—Cos of the murders you dummy.

—Josie, this is dangerous! Mr Hell is an alleged reptilian psychopath!

—Then you two should get along, like, totally famously . . .

The two made their way towards the farm house. Tom had no idea what Josie was trying to achieve but forced himself to go in order to keep his side of the bargain. Walking behind the girl, he thought about how easy it would be to kill Josie. She hadn't expressed any fear towards Tom; she seemed comfortable letting him trail behind her.

Tom thought there must be something in that kind of trust.

They approached the porch. Suddenly, Tom noticed Josie frozen in her tracks. He peered over her shoulder and saw something floating over them like a mirage.

A tall being, stooped in shadow. It had the look of an old sawbones. Hatch-marks on its fingers showed in the moonlight as it came into view. It was Mr Hell...

Hell had been snorting something, it spangled his top lip like powdered sugar. He didn't seem embarrassed about it.

—Little late for trespassing, don't ya think?

Tom and Josie were frozen to the spot. Mr Hell plucked an apple from one of the under-branches and held it aloft by the burr-knot. He presented it to Tom, who reluctantly took it and scrutinised the offering.

—Eat it—Hell insisted.

Tom took a big bite. It tasted good, crisp with a subtle dryness.

—What'd you think?

Through the fear, Tom's face was a beaming plate of joy. Hell took this as his answer. Josie was still studying the old man's face with an architect's eye. Scars overlapped on both cheeks and he had one eyebrow missing. Hell's face was like a Halloween mask, and a tatty looking one at that. Tom noticed his ancient ugliness too; he was everything expectation and dread promised. Had his apples not been so delicious he would've surely turned and ran. Tom saw the same blank stare present in most of the other antagonists in his life; Leo, Mr Alhazred, Suzie when she smirked . . .

—Pruned in winter while the trees are dormant and thinned to perfection. This orchard is my life.

Tom was still crunching his apple, trying to savour its taste. Hell knelt down to meet the two teenagers at eye level. When he spoke his breath smelled of soil and natural decay. He focused his stare on Tom.

—It's all I have.

—More than some—Josie added.

—I've been banished from the place I used to call home.

—Why?

Hell twisted his neck until the sinew looked ready to snap. It eventually made a loud crack that made Tom wince.

—I know about you...

—Know about what?—Tom took an instinctive step backwards. There were traces of the sweet apple still on his tongue.

—Help me . . . —Hell asked with his limpid, pleading eyes.

—Help you? To do what?

—Think about it, what are you good at?

—I dunno, not much! Math, science maybe? I don't know a single thing about working in an orchard . . .

—Killing women, that's what you're best at. I'm no good at it. It's the Teiidae you see. I haven't got the nerve to disobey ancient values like that, but you can summon the anger and resentment needed to extinguish a female life.

Josie snorted and muttered under her breath.

—You believe that do you?—she spoke to Hell, who continued to ignore her.

THE STATEMENT OF TOM TRYOUT

—I can only kill children, adult males, and small animals. Women are the final hurdle. I can't kill them, they all seem so maternal to me.

—That's because of the Teiidae, right?—Josie asked.

—It's a sneaky female trick, plucking feeling from the foulest of souls.

—What makes you think I can do it?? I can't kill women!—Tom protested.

Mr Hell gave Tom a knowing grin—he knew, but *how* did he know?

—You are talented boy, I can sense it in you. You can kill and consume flesh like a true monster of the night.

Tom felt pride swell inside of him then considered its source. Hell inched closer, nudging Josie out of the way. He spoke in a faint whisper.

—They used to mock me too you know.

—Who? The Gangles?

—The Gangles, women, people, all of them . . .

—Why do you want to kill women?

—The truth of the matter, is that I want this town culled. I want *us* to take it back...

—From the Gangles?

—From the Gangles *and* the people who live there. The stretch of land isn't rightfully theirs, it belongs to us. The Old Ones bequeathed it to our people centuries ago. The town went by a different name back then; The Nameless City, we can call it The Nameless City . . .

Tom looked sceptical.

—The birds sense our reptilian ancestry. They can taste our darkness like rotten maggots in their saliva. We were forced to retreat to underground chambers until there was only a few of us left . . . and the people living there right now are all hooked up to the same virtual reality headset, intruders one and all. It's time we woke them up . . .

Tom felt uncomfortable for a moment when he thought about his father or Mr Kowalski coming to harm.

—The Gangles don't like our people, we are the reptiles. The sea was once receded, there was no pier. The Nameless City was like a desert.

—Am *I* a reptile?—Josie asked, half kidding. Hell kept talking as if he hadn't even heard her.

—This is all I have left boy, growing Adam's fruit . . .

Tom could see the white fiends gathered on the roof, listening. Hell clutched the boy by the shoulders, his long fingernails subtly penetrating Tom's flesh through fabric.

—The birds, they shit on everything, take what they want, just like those fuckin townsfolk! If you don't fit in they leer at you, they can sense how weak we have become! The gulls are attracted to the stench of humanity, of servility and slovenliness, that's why they allow those people to live there. Every organism of reptilian lineage in Shaver Point is considered a trespasser, doomed for a life of utter misery.

—Jesus—Josie was ready to leave. Tom saw the flung arrows of her expression but was unmoved.

—Let me tell you something. There is a battle going on out there, between the oppressed and the oppressors. What's your name?

—Tom . . .

—Tom, you know what it feels like to be oppressed don't you?

—I guess . . .

—And what about your little girlfriend, does she know oppression?

—I'm not his girlfriend—Josie said, snapping to attention. She seemed a little agitated that Hell was only now acknowledging her existence.

Hell's eyeballs ping-ponged around in their sockets.

—I'll deal with the children and animals, I'll give you some salt bags to fend off the Gangles. When they eat salt their heads explode. Tom, you can take the women. I'll capture them one by one and you expunge them accordingly.

Tom's head ache returned. Hell stood up from his kneeling position.

—You're getting migraines . . .

—I get them a lot.

—It's the Gangle siren that does that. It's how they hurt us.

Josie butted in—Okay, this is just getting kind of, like, fucked up now. Tom, it's one thing to kill some cheerleader slut, but killing the women of Shaver Point? I mean . . . *really*?

—Every man has his palms run through with nails—Hell looked straight at Josie when he said this.

—Stop! Stop saying shit! Tom, you're not really gonna, like, listen to this nutjob are ya?

Hell put his hands on Tom's shoulders and spoke to him as a father would his only son.

—You want to belong to something ancient and great? Show me what you can do . . .

Tom turned to Josie.

—What, you think you're some kind of fucking Holden character now? Out to kill the phonies, right?

—The phonies . . .

—Tom . . .

He advanced on the girl, grasping the slender column of her throat with strangler's hands, bearing down on her until her legs bent and she began to fall backwards. They wrestled on the ground for a few minutes, Josie's nails tearing into Tom's wrists . . . Tom thumbing the larynx until Josie started making rasping sounds, a final cry to the Gangles for help . . . until she finally submitted to him.

Hell stood still, frozen with pride and shock.

—She was a Gangle . . . you heard her make that sound.

Tom released his grip and Josie's head fell limp. He *did* have a migraine again.

—It's all cultural conditioning. The people of Shaver Point are as cruel as the Gangles; they have a mentality of privilege, subjugation and wanting to dominate . . .

Tom knelt in the dirt next to Josie and resigned himself to his inescapable destiny. He belonged here, even if he felt cold and alone on the inside. That might never go away. His temples pulsed and two veins branched off down either side of Tom's face, his brain opening for the first time, skull separating, nose breathing in the fetid stench of murder and savouring it in his throat, in his heart, in his viscera eyes . . .

ANOTHER UNINSPIRED, POORLY WRITTEN METAPHOR FOR SOMETHING NO ONE CARES ABOUT, OKAY . . .

THESE DAYS HE just couldn't understand a single word she said. She thought he wasn't listening, but he was—or maybe he just wasn't listening hard enough, depending on how you look at it . . .

Bee opened her mouth and a silent word fell out. Terry sat on the edge of the bed and pulled up his jeans. He asked Bee to repeat what she just said. She opened her mouth and, once again, only a muted gasp emerged. Bee's face looked pained when she saw Terry's confounded expression, as if she'd said exactly what she wanted to say and he *still* wasn't getting it. She stood up and stared at him across the bed. She made a serious face, pointed to her mouth (as if to say *READ MY LIPS*) and started forming the shapes of what words were supposed to sound like. Terry still heard nothing. She pointed to her own ears, begging him to listen closely.

—I'm sorry Bee, I got nothin'.

The girl threw her hands in the air, blew her

cheeks in exasperation. Fractals of light came through the shades and stretched out in an intense stillness. Terry tried to explain.

—I know you're talkin' but I honestly got nothin' . . .

Bee ran into the bathroom and slammed the door shut. Terry climbed over the bed and pressed his ear to the door.

—Bee, honey, just try and make a sound ok?

Nothing.

—I can see you're trying to say something to me and, by Christ I want to know, believe me I want to know! Is this about Mephisto? This isn't some game to make you feel dumb, believe me . . .

Nothing.

—Bee, we've been married for four years and I've always been able to hear you. The minute we stop understanding each other is the day we go get a divorce, right?

Terry had said this with the intention of being funny and intentionally melodramatic but it prompted the smashing of a mirror instead.

—Bee? Bee is everything ok?

Terry paced the room for a few minutes then decided he'd have to ram the door in. He took one big run-up from the door at the other side of the room and shoulder-barged his way into the bathroom. The lock on the door snapped clean off, the jamb splintered. Bee was sitting on the edge of the bath with her face buried in her palms. Terry went over to her and knelt to her level. He noticed the shards of glass all over the bathroom floor reflecting back a distorted portrait of the couple. Terry swallowed hard and placed a hand on his wife's shoulder. She shrugged him off.

—Bee, honey, I love you, do you understand what I'm saying?

Bee was unresponsive. This all felt like some white-water dream.

—You know, it's true what they say about a person, that they die twice. Once when they stop breathing and again when the last person they knew says their name for the last time. As long as you're around whatever Mephisto stood for will still be . . . alive.

Until now, he'd always been able to win her over. Terry realised the full seriousness of the situation for the first time. Bee opened her mouth again but was choked back with tears. She gave up trying and ran out of the bathroom and back into the bedroom. Terry got up slowly, almost completely defeated, and followed after her. She was scribbling something down on a pad with a make-up pen.

—What are you writing?

Bee held the pad over so he could read her message. Terry screwed up his eyes then stood up straight like he had a pole up his ass.

The pad read—**I CAN'T UNDERSTAND YOU!**

A PAIR SO RAPED

They say the creature clutched her by the arms
Until the timber of her delicate bones
Began to splinter and crack and sing
It whispered awful things, masculine things
Into her in some soft bastard language,
Not Latin, but not dissimilar
Mind like a steel trap
The rape of HER was a travesty
A monster's spoil of war, **taken**
Taken, taken, taken, taken, taken, taken
HE *TOOK* her
She had been scarred through from mind, body to
    soul.
She also suffered persistent gynaecological problems.
The rape of HIM was an embarrassment
To a patriarchal society
'Is he still a husband?
Isn't he now a wife?
How can he protect me?
How can I ever feel protected again?'
Wandering the chiaroscuro through the smoky
    sfumato
Head jacked on its axle
Looking ever up at the dizzying ablaq above

A PAIR SO RAPED

Ribs of rock
Leathern eyelids
A chrysalis . . .

BAPTIZM OF FIRE

"Our flag shall be a symbol
That truth and justice reign,
In peace or battle honour'd,
And this we count as gain,
To hand on to our children
A banner without stain."

Nigeria We Hail Thee (1960-1978)

OBI BAMGBALA WALKED through the parched suburbs of Old Lagos.

The streets pulsed with activity to the beat of the boy's frenzied heartbeat. Since his emancipation from the Slave State, Obi had struggled to settle into the city. Although he had escaped work in a forced labour enclave, he had entered into a new world of servitude, where society had been weakened by greed and poverty.

Obi watched the people go through the motions, like a clockwork colony of insects—folks carried baskets of cloths and trays of food to their respective stalls—a file of cruisers and tandem mope heads clogged the lanes; by the wayside, groups of scammers negotiated in various ancient dialects that were unfamiliar to Obi.

He did not yet know this world.

All the clamouring voices startled the young boy at first. Under the Slave State's watchful eye, Old Lagos was an intimidating authority, but soon Obi noticed the comparisons with his old city of Okpella in Edo State. Often the marketplace was of similar discontent. He came to realise that every strange fruit or herb sold in Lagos was something he had seen many times before back home. Obi delighted, as he had done in Okpella, at the vast range of antiques, jewellery and crafts. On Sunday, Obi and his aunt would buy from the booths—Egusi, rice, pounded yams, satchels of banga soup paste, fried plantain for Dodo and delicious fruit called agbalumo.

While the former capital bustled with an impatient commotion, in a way it was comparable to the Yoruba drummers who marched the markets beating their talking hourglasses. Lagos music was just a more acquired taste. Edo market itself was located beside the deafening Benin Abuja Road. Obi did not take long in adapting.

Doctor Chopin, a vicious and insane surgeon, was after him.

Chopin would *love* to see Obi on his gurney with a wasted heart . . .

Apart from avoiding Chopin, his is reason for being in Old Lagos was that he was to attend university there. He had been unconditionally accepted to study botany after achieving the necessary B4 in fishery and chemistry and a notable A3 credit with distinction in biology. The Slave State had previously only allowed Austria-German, New Catalonian, and Soviet Asian nations to enroll its people in higher education, however Baroness Un soon realised that as long as the main hub of humanity in the South and West were deprived of their basic amenities, then there was really no honest threat—and so why *not* allow Afro-Oceanic nations that same right?

Obi's father was a farmer in Okpella, as well as an affiliate of the Benin tribe and a long time contributor to the State—this is how Obi escaped the enclaves.

Going to university was something he respected his son for doing. Before setting off for Old Lagos, his father warned him to stick to his studies, beware of Chopin, and avoid getting caught up in the growing number of vicious anti-Slave state confraternities that were swarming the universities. He told of the wandering Mephisto and its ability to tempt honest men and women, of the ugly Winged Shaver Gangles and their reptilian nemesis, locked in an eternal feud in the South Eastern extremities of the Slave State mainland. Obi promised to respect his father's wishes.

The boy browsed through some beautifully designed but illegally smuggled wax resist textiles, in two minds whether to part with his money. He opted not to contribute to a dishonest cause.

***

Standing ankle deep in a shallow reservoir in Epe's coastal market, Obi bought some fish food packets from two grateful husband and wife peddlers. They wished him well on his journey. Pig-faced children scuffled hard in the silvery streets, troughs piling high, awful slander spoken in barbed oinking. Trash cans overflow/Wednesday summer heat send lines of reeking flesh up into the swirling vortex-hole where the sun used to be before it fell out of the sky and into the ocean. Women wept the eternal ballad, histrionic moans—sounds of nightmare trains rumbling on the distant track of thinking . . .

Once the boy had arrived outside the gates of the school, Obi saw an attractive older girl waiting with a collection of textbooks clutched close to her chest. The very fact she was older gave her instant motherly appeal. She seemed approachable, and since Obi did not know anyone here yet, he thought about an introduction. He nervously presented himself to the girl.

—Hello. My name is Obi Bamgbala. I don't really know anyone here.

To his relief the girl smiled sympathetically.

—That's ok. I'm Asa. It's very nice to meet you Obi Bamgbala.

Beneath the confidence of her voice and the poise of her carriage, Asa's face reddened.

—You're in your first year?

—Yes, how did you know?

—You look absolutely terrified.

Asa giggled, covering the arc of her smile with a red jotter. Her red broche, festooned by white, yellow disc floret daisies, mesmerised Obi as she gestured with her hands erratically. She continued to reassure him.

—Don't worry. We'll look after you.

—Thank you. I need to find my dorm room first.

—Come with me little one.

—I appreciate this, Asa.

He wondered if she knew he was smitten. Very probably. Woman were sensitive to male infatuation; Obi knew this because he often found himself infatuated with someone or other.

As she led Obi into the halls of residence, a completely new landscape seemed to present itself. Coating the surrounding walls of the ghetto passageway, scribbles of graffiti filled the new dweller of Lagos State with discouragement. Unfriendly promises from local gangs helped mark their territory. Obi read some of what was inscribed on the stone corridors.

"We go kill all Ijaw people
with our gun"

"The end shall never come until
the beginning has come and pass
away"

"Pyrates stay away"

"This is the end of Egbesu
in Odi village."

"Anything goes up most come
down this is the end of
Egbesu"

"Say no to Odi"

"Viscera eyes inside you"

Those responsible for the graffiti seemed to belong to the confraternities his father had warned him about. Beside each threat, there were signatures. Altogether, there must have been over twenty street and creek gang monikers. The rumbling discontent was a strange phenomenon. Each gang was passionately anti-Slave State, but could not agree amongst themselves. The best jobs for a slave involved working for officials rolling pats of butter, boiling Baroness Un's eggs, pounding ice, or grinding coffee. However, the majority found themselves down the mine shafts. Obi reminded himself how lucky he was to be here . . .

Those from the overtly masculine gangs (The Outlaws, Second Sons of Satan, Brotherhood of Blood, Buccaneers, Red Sea Horse, Icelanders, and the Black Axe) outnumbered the few female led ones (Daughters of Jezebel, Amazons, The Black Bras). Obi saw for the first time that although the former nation of Nigeria was economically prosperous, its people still lived in civil unrest—especially students who desired higher education.

The university had looked so promising from the outside.

***

Asa acknowledged the wall art, though only briefly.

—You must be very careful little one. There are people here which you must avoid at all costs.

Obi ached to ask further questions but sensed he should choose to discuss something less serious with Asa instead. Obi experienced feelings for the girl he'd never had before.

At the entrance hall Asa stopped.

—This is the hall of residence access. Just go up the stairs and find the room that matches your ticket. And be sure to avoid a boy who calls himself Ogu. He's the leader of the Black Axe. He's an engineer student but claims to be the reincarnated ancestral spirit of Olorun. Please be careful. I will keep a watch on you after classes.

Obi thanked Asa once again for her assistance. He plucked up the courage to ask her out.

—Would you maybe want to go for a drink sometime?

—I'm allergic to alcohol.

He saw the intrinsic fear of castration in her sex, the dread certainty of her eventual death. Obi produced a Jam Cap that a flogger gave him in the city centre. He was too afraid to use it alone. Asa seemed unnerved by the materialisation of drugs.

—I better go!

He watched her leave down the main steps, captivated by her flow. Her long wiry fingers clung to the handrail as she floated delicately to the bottom like a wonderful guiding apparition—but once Asa came to the passageway, Obi forgot about any implications her charity may have brought. A tall, charismatic boy with a perfect face and broad shoulders greeted her like a lover. Crouching to her level, the boy started kissing around Asa's mouth. To Obi the display seemed to last an eternity.

Disheartened by the girl's devotion to another man, Obi Bamgbala crawled away to his dark dorm room to weep. The dumb hunger of lust made things even more complicated. He heard the students fucking in the surrounding dorms—a gymnasium of bodies murdering each other, the dead screwing the dead.

He felt Dr Chopin's eyes on him, waiting for the *SNAPPING*, *POPPING*, *BURSTING* sound of his heart . . .

***

The wallpaper around him sweated from the walls. He forced open a window from its latch and stuck his head out for air. A crowd of insects attacked the boy, magnetised to the oily moisture of his cheeks and forehead. Tears were all around him, the aqueous layer and eternal epiphora. He drank from a bottle of water and his thirst was abated. Suddenly his despair diminished.

Tomorrow was his first day at Old Lagos University and Obi was looking forward to it.

Obi had yet to witness the brutality he'd been told was rife in Lagos State. He knew students were rebelling against it all (because, of course, a decent education did not exclude you from a message from the Slave State), but Obi found it curious that the violence hadn't yet spilled into his path. Obi was famous for inviting trouble. On his way to the first botany class of the semester, the boy kept a sharp eye for anyone who might seek to harm him.

Sitting in a seat by a single desk, Obi began to unpack his equipment for the class. He was the first person there, which was completely his intention. Obi had been in class a few minutes before he saw there were hardly any students in the lecture theatre; he was even more surprised to find that the sparse collection of students at the beginning of the lesson didn't pick up, even as the lecturer arrived, ready to give his seminar.

The lecturer introduced himself as Mr. Abayomi. Everything about him radiated knowledge and wisdom; he looked like something from a phantasmagorical dream. At ninety-five he had avoided enrolment in the enclaves. People began speculating that he was a Slave State mole. No one could believe a man could last so long without being taken into forced labour.

Only halfway through his lecture Obi knew he was going to enjoy this class. Abayomi carried an old-fashioned blackboard pointer and when he spoke of an area of study that excited him, he would thrash the stick against the desk in front of him. His enthusiasm was inspiring and infectious. The boy felt like he was beginning to realise his true passion and before long, among the meagre numbers of the lecture theatre, he rose straight to the head of the class.

In the coming few days, Obi had little trouble with his university life. He spent most of his time in his dorm room. He'd seen Asa with her boyfriend but kept his composure. There had been no violence to speak of. Women and men danced merrily through the night in room and parlour huts. Everyone seemed courteous. At university, his studies in Mr. Abayomi's class were proving increasingly rewarding; the teacher would test the boy in ways he thought might throw a simple freshman, but Obi had read well under his guidance and always responded with intelligent solutions.

Abayomi told him to beware the grey goo of the Slave State. The self-replicators who sift the mined materials, who crowd the biosphere, who eat the environment and destroy all carbon-based life instead of just the hydrocarbons in the oil.

Obi was fascinated by his teacher's literary career in Shell County, and after class each afternoon Abayomi would share stories from his time as an editor.

—Since the holocaust, which actually came to me in a precognitive dream months before, everyone wanted to write their autobiography. Everyone had their own perspective on the disaster and of the resulting outbreak which saw each man, woman, and child in Shell County turned into a hideous reanimated monster. As an editor that's a really dull way to make a living . . .

Abayomi had avoided the worst of the outbreak but experienced the most toxic nature of people.

—What?

—Back when I edited for Subterfuge I was a real highflyer. I wrote his biography and in return he removed me from the conscription line.

—Brilliant! My family is also immune from conscription.

Although they were only a few days into the first semester Obi was enjoying class and relishing his relationship with Abayomi. Agronomy was his favourite subject.

2.

DAY FOUR ON campus saw everything he had been forewarned about become reality for the first time. After leaving the dorm one morning, Obi spotted a group of students surrounding another youth. Hiding behind the border of the Lagos State signpost he spied what was going on. All of the students crowding around the boy wore black bandanas and carried machetes. One boy started sermonising.

—You are a female sympathiser! They have no visible genitals and yet you continue to pursue them? You are afraid of the place of immanence, the outré, the body without organs.

They poked their weapons into the centre of the circle. One boy stood dominant just out of the way of any danger. He was clearly the leader, the orchestrator of this cruel crescendo. Obi could not take his eyes from this boy. He knew instantly it was Ogu, the engineer student and first in command of the ill-reputed Black Axe cult. Ogu wore a weathered "Scarface" t-shirt and had a long black fringe which overhung his bandana, hiding the left side of his face. He was scourged with acne but was good-looking.

As the mob separated, the target of their carnage

came into view. In the middle of the dust bowl quarry beside the university, the bloody remains of Asa's boyfriend lay motionless. He'd been beaten and hacked to death in broad daylight, then was to be left like road kill for some unsuspecting student to stumble across. Ogu stepped up to the limp, disjointed cadaver and knelt to its level as if he were still among the living. Ogu began to talk like a judge declaring a guilty verdict.

—Wilson Chinualumgu. You have been executed accordingly for rallying against the Black Axe movement. For campaigning against anti-Slave State cultists and for copulation with one village whore, Asa Taiwo. Your final punishment—decapitation, then public piking. The viscera eyes judge you . . . "

Ogu retrieved a machete from a crony and proceeded to saw off Wilson Chinualumgu's head.

Obi couldn't look away. He thought he'd be disgusted, and he was, but something compelled him to keep watching. It was Ogu's level-headedness which had the boy stuck. Obi found the respect he had for this merciless killer surpassed even that of his admiration for Mr Abayomi.

After chopping at Wilson's neck for a few minutes, he had finally managed to disengage the skull. Ogu held the head high above his head like some glorious sports trophy. He smiled as the dangling spinal-cord dripped fluid and flapped loosely. Ogu and the rest of the Black Axe rejoiced by kicking the severed head around the road like a grotesque football. They screamed—Ayei Axmen!—triumphantly. Those around who witnessed the murder did nothing. In fact, once the boys were out of sight everyone resumed as normal.

Obi could think of going to only one person—
Asa—but didn't want to be the one who broke the
tragic news of her lover's death. The boy found he had
no desires to report the incident or find council in the
arms of a sympathetic adult. Obi was far from
traumatised. What he felt was more akin to that of an
awakening; he wanted to talk to someone about how
impressively Ogu conducted himself, about how
ruthless and inspiring he'd found the whole
experience. Obi held him in the same regard as action
movie anti-heroes like Rambo or the Terminator.
Even the Al Pacino t-shirt he sported seemed
representative of his vigour and guile.

***

The next day the school gate wore the head of
Wilson Chinualumgu, his face contorted and frozen
with those final few agonised thoughts. Needless to
say, Asa had been trying to reach Wilson the night he
was murdered by the Black Axe. Now her worst fears
were realised as she came into the building early that
morning. When she saw his head carved up and
served like an obscene entrée' on Lagos State's rusted
fence pole, she sank to her knees and did not return
to her feet until a military policeman threatened her.

Obi left Asa alone for a couple of days after the
incident. As much as he longed to console her with
the false intention of making her his girlfriend, his
father had taught restraint persistently when he was
growing up. It wouldn't be appropriate to make
advancements on the recently bereaved. In truth, Obi
had begun to resent the notion of compassion and the
conduct that came with it. To Obi, it seemed his father
taught concepts that deliberately denied all pleasure.
The senseless murder of Wilson had little effect on

Obi Bamgbala, other than that it stimulated a dark spirit inside of him. It occurred to Obi that what he respected about Ogu and the Black Axe was their complete *lack* of restraint and compassion. They fought for only one principle ideology, and that was self-fulfilment. Like pirates, they took what they wanted, killed who they wanted, thought what they wanted—to live like Gods, servants of the State's chaos and yet independent of the State entirely. He saw how Ogu was able to kill and take revenge and go unpunished. Obi wanted to be respected like that.

A fly steered its way onto Obi's chest. It buzzed, feeling its way around the boy's knitted shirt before resting its wings and becoming stationary. Obi observed the insect for a moment. The jagged mandible of its mouth caught on the wool of his garment and the tiny insect was suddenly trapped. No matter how hard it flapped around, it was stuck. Obi mercifully slammed the broad lane of his palm over its struggling body, crushing the insect to death. The boy saw its last frantic motions. He felt nothing. Even the final backward march of the fly to the gravel beneath, Obi remained unperturbed.

In class all he thought about was Ogu. Even as Abayomi came in to explain the gruesome death of the student union head, a task he took great discomfort in doing, Obi fantasised. This would be the first botany class Obi Bamgbala coasted through. At the end of the lecture Mr. Abayomi kept him behind to inquire as to why he was so uncharacteristically quiet during his lesson.

—Obi, what's troubling you?

—Nothing—lied the boy.

—Come on, don't give me that!

—I'm fine.

While Obi didn't initially enjoy being disrespectful to his cherished tutor, there was a defiance he found pleasure in. Abayomi was an agent of repression, a holocaust profiteer. His coldness was the rejection of comfort and conformity. Obi suddenly found himself wishing to disassociate from the comfort Abayomi gave him.

—Obi, you just don't seem yourself today.

—No sir, today I believe I have finally discovered who and what I wish to be.

—Men fight for their servitude as stubbornly as though it were their salvation.

Abayomi coiled the pointed tip of his beard around his finger, considering the change present in the boy. He delivered one last piece of advice disguised as proverb.

—A chicken that scratches at the dung hill will soon find its mother's thigh bones.

Obi was unmoved. The teacher became suddenly quiet. Obi knew he had succeeded in alienating the old man. Then, without saying another word to each other, the apprentice left his teacher behind.

***

Outside the university, Obi's new idol could be seen with a throng of Black Axe mafia lagging behind their leader keenly. Ogu was still wearing his shabby Scarface shirt but possessed the same imposing presence. It seemed the Black Axe had a problem with another detractor of their organisation. This time it was a boy Obi did not know.

Ogu strode forward; the boy he advanced towards had backed himself into a corner between the step and a small alley. Sweat and tears bombarded the boy's face as he begged for his life. Ogu again read his verdict.

—Ucheoma Kālu, you are guilty of disrespect. You are born from a family of whores and bastards and Slave State informants. I curse your name. I curse your existence. You will be sad. You will be alone. You will die before you're twenty-one.

Ogu pulled something from his trouser belt, a wand composed of fetishised caves of skull and bone wrapped around a thick raffia palm cane. The stick clattered with beaded stones that were held inside. As Ogu chanted, he shook it inches from Kālu's sweat-saturated face. To Obi's amazement the act of "juju" seemed to be having its effect on the boy. Kālu quaked in fear while his extrasensory dominator tried to force the lock of his soul to embed his curse. Obi was surprised by the Black Axe leader's mercy. Not a day ago he'd seen Ogu decapitate another human-being like a farmer tearing away at his livestock in preparation for October's agricultural yield. The gang laughed at their victim's frailness before Ogu craned his neck one last time to spit in the direction of Kālu.

Obi approached the boy as he struggled up the main steps.

—Hi. Are you all right?

Obi, in his new state of mind detested the false, snivelling pretences.

—Yes—Trembled Kālu—He had a grey woollen jumper on but it didn't mask the fact he was savagely thin.

—Why did they attack you?

—I owe them money.

—Why?

—Why do you care?

—I just do . . .

—Ogu's father was a simple native of Ogoni, mine was an oil worker, mining petroleum in the River Niger Delta. Eventually he was promoted to ICE-9 manager and supervisor of other thin films and interfaces. I am in debt to him because of how the NNPC and Slave State has supposedly treated the locals of his area. But I will not pay. I have no money to do so.

—Why doesn't he kill you?

—He will eventually. He has cursed me with his black magic.

—How did he come to be in the gang?

—He's been in it since his first semester. Ogu was once a decent student but a prophet believed him to be a witch, and so was sent away by his father. I don't know anything else.

—But . . . how do people who want to be in the Black Axe go about joining?

Obi sensed now that the boy was becoming confused by his questions.

—Why would anyone want to? You need to pay them eight thousand naira for starters.

—They charge you to join?

—And that's not all they want. You have to show what you're made of. A statement of intent to prove you deserve to be in their gang.

Obi spotted a detached water duct. He walked over to salvage it with the purpose of making his defining statement to the Black Axe.

The decision was easier than he originally anticipated. Obi dropped the metal cylinder onto the unsuspecting Kālu's head. Fragments of bone broke away from the skull and by the end of the beating Obi was covered in Ucheoma Kālu's brain fluid. With great relish Obi smeared the blood of his kill over his face and turned to see if Ogu and the Black Axe had seen him. It hadn't matter to the boy that those around him condemned his actions with shared disgust, for Ogu and the gang *had* witnessed the murder.

—What do you think you're doing?—Ogu posed.

—I . . . —Obi hesitated as his idol approached, mesmerised. His eyes were milky, substance-packed, full of viscera. There was a scar that traced from his cheek to his neck that had scabbed over like spun sugar.

—You WHAT?—Ogu's aggressive tone hurried the boy into response.

—I did this . . . for **you**.—Spluttered Obi.

—For me?—Scoffed the commander to his fleet. The Black Axe boys cackled. Ogu straightened up his smile before answering back.

—And why did you do this for *me,* freshman?

—I want to be in the Black Axe

Again the group of boys erupted with laughter. Ogu silenced them with a raised hand.

—You can't just "join" the Axeneb

—Oh, I know . . . but I'd do anything.

Ogu looked interested by the loyalty Obi was willing to supply him with.

—You can kill—He gestured to Ucheoma Kālu's lifeless body—But how do you feel after it? Can you do it again?

Without a trace of doubt Obi replied—Yes I could. I *live* to fucking kill.

—"I live to kill? Hmm . . . I like that. I cursed that

traitor with "juju", and the Gods sent me you to devour him.

Obi beamed with pride.

—Do you have the money to go with your balls freshman?

—I can get the money.

—You want to be MY slave? I mean, MINE, ME . . . not a slave of the State. You'll be emancipated from serfdom and reinstated as my personal bitch. You want that?

—Yes...

—*His own mind has turned on him. This kind of guilt and forced repression is incredibly dangerous. It's almost like he's succumbed to the baser impulses of thought, training himself to become something, preparing himself for something . . .*

***

The medical college students emptied. Obi waited patiently for Ogu's arrival. He should have been in horticulture class.

When the final body had evacuated the building, from around the corner came the Black Axe. Ogu halted his group and swaggered to Obi.

—Well done on being here on time. It's good you can be punctual.

—Thank you Ogu—grovelled the boy. However, despite his gracious intentions, Obi had unknowingly angered the commander.

—Thank you, yes, fuckin thank you! Thank ME, ME! D'you know this scar, **this** fuckin scar, huh? I shot myself, or tried to . . . the shot turned out not to be fatal . . . d'you know what I said to my devastated mother . . . what I'd intended as my last request?

—No . . .

—That she fetch me a mirror so I could watch myself die like a fuckin man . . .

Obi stood silently.

—I assume you don't have the eight thousand naira yet?

—Not just yet sir.

—Well you can get me something as collateral. I'm giving you one chance; succeed and you will progress to the next stage of initiation.

—Anything—he reassured humbly.

—Asa Taiwo. You will bring her to me by sundown tomorrow evening.

—Of course sir.

Ogu's cruel yellow eyes were like a reptile's. No matter how obliging his new disciple seemed to be, Ogu continued to leer like a child focusing the sun into a magnifying glass over an unassuming ant. And that's what Obi felt like—an insect. He perhaps expected his induction to be glorious, but he had since felt anything but.

Ogu dismissed the boy and returned to the Black Axe.

Obi hadn't spoken to Asa since her boyfriend was murdered. Approaching her was difficult. She still possessed that same warmth and glow even as she collected her books sadly from the library. Her empty stare told of a heart-breaking reality. Obviously pre-occupied by Wilson's untimely end, Asa barely reacted at all to Obi's greeting.

—Yes. Hello little one. How are you?—Asa spoke softly and with more than a hint of distance in her gaze.

—I've been fine. I'm very sorry about . . .

—Please don't. Don't say his name—Pleaded the

girl as a solitary jewel of moisture dashed down her cheek, leaving a trail in its wake.

—I'm sorry Asa. I actually came to ask you for help. Mr. Abayomi wants students to pick a post-grad tutor to help them in research—his face not meeting her eye—will you be mine?

—I'd be happy to—her face displayed its first signs of hope. Obi had succeeded in duping the mourning girl. He could not deny that he felt bad; Asa was the only person who had shown him kindness when he first arrived, but the Black Axe were all that mattered to him now. His employment meant the world to him.

As Obi guided Asa into the Black Axe's lair, the girl became curious.

—Why have you taken me this way? I thought all post-grad tuition had to take place in a teacher's class?

Before Obi had the chance to lie, Ogu turned the bend and into sight. He smirked knowingly in her direction. She realised quickly the young boy's deception.

—Oh Obi . . . —she wheezed desolately. Asa was then led into the hostel. Four Axe members carried her limply as the girl wept in hopeless despair. Her thin forearms were held securely between two sets of thick bestial clamps. Dragging her feet along the sand, Asa's head flopped in bleak submission. With no remorse for his betrayal, Obi was pleased to see Ogu satisfied with his work. He followed the group back to their enclave.

Asa was taken into a draped room. Ogu addressed Obi without looking at him. After loosening his jeans and then his underpants he explained what the boy would come to expect.

—You have done well maggot. Captain Cannibal will explain to you the stages involved in passing your *jolly* INI. He is strong breed.

Ogu pointed to a brutish boy who wore white regalia and the confraternity headband. His face was stern but Obi swallowed his fear. Ogu unashamedly exposed his buttocks, then entered the draped chamber completely naked. It was clear he was going to rape Asa. Obi was surprised how little he cared. Captain Cannibal then picked up where his master had left off, elaborating the specifics of the gruelling initiation procedures.

—First I will give you your interview. You will then come with me to "the island" where you will undergo a series of tests in which you will have to prove your manhood to Ogu. Should you succeed, there will be a celebratory ceremony.

Obi shook with excitement. Spotting a 50-caliber M2 machine gun that rested in the corner of the room, Obi was compelled to ask questions.

—Where do you get your weapons?

—We get our guns from Akwa blacksmiths. We find ourselves with replicas of those used in the Biafran conflict so are well equipped with the best defences. There's no intergalactic Slave State bullshit in our battalion . . .

—Don't you worry you will be caught?

—No. We are funded by River State House of Assembly. A movement through which we exchange oil for arms. Some of our soldiers even go on to work for the MEND and we work closely with similar military organisations. We are not simply a "street and creek" operation as you may have heard. We are neo-terrorists who have divine prevalence. We live by the law of the jungle and train in ancient common tactics of physical combat.

—This sounds so . . . —Obi's enthusiasm was not well received by Captain Cannibal who proceeded to cut him off half way. Cannibal was young in the face; he had wiry hair and a bad complexion of craters and divots.

—Speak less boy. Else I will cut out your tongue.

Obi shut his mouth firm in embarrassment.

—On the dead man's hour you will meet me on the "island" for your interview.

Captain Cannibal instructed his new recruit to leave and rendezvous at Bar Beach.

3.

IN OBI'S DREAMS he was a slave . . .

Baroness Un stood there with his small penis resting on the palm of his hand. Obi took off all its clothes and stood before him, face shamed, shoulders hunched up to his jaw-line, both hands covering his own sex. Shifting iotas of light ignited the tight, pink flesh of his legs in the darkened room. Un's mellifluous jelly surged with excitement as the human's fear became apparent. The Baroness said something in an alien tongue and squinted through the awning.

—Did you hear about the dust explosion?—Un asked.

Obi nodded.

—They think it was an elevator cage at shaft three that fell onto the pit head, but more likely it was the ignition of methane by an exposed flame.

Obi had been hewing sulphur by hand all day and wore the scars of his labour. A streak of dried blood weaved down to his left pectoral. Un strummed the visible tendons beneath the human's wound.

—I know you had family in that shaft, a son?

Obi just quivered in fear and sorrow.

—You know, on most planets your position here would be considered quite privileged.

Obi gave a gargled response on account of his tongue being removed. Un chose to ignore the animosity of its tone. He placed a clammy hand to the back of the human's neck and pulled him in, pushing an eager tongue into its mouth. The kiss ended with a wet SLAP sound and Obi's mouth came away swathed in alien sputum that reflected like the spectral lines of mercury.

—You people mine rock salt, gravel and clay, remove over-burden and debris . . . power up the arrastra . . . but you have other uses.

The astonishing truth was that Un had love in his heart, sunken buried treasure that no one could stomach unearthing, to obtain his hidden wealth of heart. It was because no one would ever seek him out that he so frequently gave in to repugnant appetites. Even Obi sensed the goodness within such intrinsic, ugly evil.

Un noticed that he was malnourished looking, every stark bone in his body visible through a thin lycra of flesh. He had once been a junky, a Jam-Capper; the malocclusion of his teeth gave that away. Un threw Obi a leg, shin to foot, and told him to eat it, enjoy it. Without a second's consideration he had seized the primal cut and savagely mauled at its sinew. It didn't occur to Obi that the leg might've once belonged to a former co-worker, a friend, a family member, a teacher . . .

—It's quite illegal, *this* I mean; it's considered repugnant.

Obi was so consumed by the part of his dream where he ate the flesh of his loved ones that he didn't hear the dialogue vividly.

—We're considered asexual for the most part, not

fornicators. Sex is considered a rather humiliating ritual. We get more pleasure out of defecation, the strain, the evacuation process . . . the intense relief expulsion. Defecation is much more a practice of pleasure than necessity. We don't have the genitals for fucking, you see. I mean, look at this measly thing— Un gestured to the shrivelled bulb in his hand—you couldn't please yourself with a reproductive tool like this, never mind satisfy another body. But we do have perfect assholes, tight, tubular . . .

When Obi even thought about this part of the dream his mouth filled up with saliva.

—But . . . since arriving in this planet, I have become better acquainted with the instant gratification your species spends entire lifetimes in search of.

Then . . .

—When eating a human being, well, it's complicated. We cannot consume the brain or spinal cord, which runs the risk of Creutzfeldt-Jakob disease. You slimy palefaces are crawling with sickness.

And . . .

—My confidante Moog advised against all this too, of course he did! He's inhaled so much hay dust and mould spores to think with any rationality. He finds human flesh stomach-churning, your physical forms, both male and female, utterly repulsive. But I must admit, *I* can see the appeal . . .

When Obi awoke he was up free again, but he missed the taste of flesh on his lips . . .

***

Bar Beach wasn't too far away for the boy to walk. He spent all day thinking about the Black Axe, preparing himself for the most important day of his life. The beach soon began to stand out. An expanse of blackened shore lined the horizon. Rows of reclining extraterrestrial holidaymakers roped a terminal contour like some open coastline morgue. Their shading umbrellas folded inside out, but were still in better condition than the tourists themselves. An accident had occurred nearby. A diesel-carrying stationery tanker collided with a luxury tour-bus— landscape of fire and mangled metal. By the shore side, the road wore a profound crater where the bus had buried itself meters below. The entry wound left scabs of vehicles and human remains by its yawning gorge. There was still the odd wheel trim or detached power train chromium-netted with the subtle pinkness of flesh. A multi-story car park almost toppled over by the speeding tankers bumping vibration, overhung the motorway gulf. The road had already been inundated with un-embanked water.

Obi felt everything sat quite elegantly like a piece of contemporary art. These images were both horrific and satisfying to him in his new state of mind. Obi felt like he was able to *wish* destruction on innocent life. Now there were less people in the city, he could see just how startlingly beautiful New Lagos was. Multitudes of sandy coves decorated the sea. Wind-milled plains further south. Disinherited of more humanity, Lagos stood on its own two feet in an overwhelmingly apocalyptic way.

Obi felt like he deserved pain and torture on a super conscious level. On an even deeper level of consciousness he'd trained his mind to repress the repository of all remembered experience—the brain stuck in a repeated pattern of conflict, the desire to punish himself and the intrinsic natural instinct of survival.

As the Nigerian police and ambulance crews rushed to the aid of those injured in the crash, Captain Cannibal signalled for Obi to come onto the beach. He was accompanied by two other Black Axe members who stood over a throbbing bonfire.

—This is Ox and Bloody Son. They will be your invigilators for your initiation. It's almost sundown. Are you ready?

Obi gulped and nodded his agreement. Families screamed in the distance.

The captain made the boy kneel. Then a cup of red ritualistic punch was handed to him. Obi was told that the drink was concocted of alcohol, blood, and Ogu's semen. The boy relished the thought of swallowing his hero's nectar. He felt virile and strong when it passed through his body.

Once that had been consumed, the captain declared:

—The boy has solidarity. But does he have resilience?

Obi's cloths were stripped from him. The boy didn't enjoy being so vulnerable and exposed when there was still a glimmer of day left. Young people sniggered at Obi's nude body. He felt infantile and pathetic. But worse was to come. Ox forced him to the ground before Captain Cannibal and Bloody Son proceeded to beat his body relentlessly. The Captain untied his belt and lashed Obi's bare back with it. None of the Black Axe held back in their vicious attack, but Obi did not release even a whimper. When Ox and Bloody Son were done kicking and punching him, the captain whipped him one last time across the face before the beating ceased. Obi was helped to his feet by the men.

—Once you have recited the Axe code of secrecy your name will be added into the secret scrolls. Repeat the following, freshman—*'I do solemnly swear to pledge my entire future to the cause of the Black Axe confraternity'.*

Obi repeated through bloody coughs.

—*'I devote my existence to the great leader Ogu for as long as I remain mortal. I love my master. I love his group. My beliefs are now that of the Black Axe and I belong to the Black Axe. Ayei Axmen!'*

Obi duly echoed his superior's oath. His painful spluttering and sombre smile betrayed the extent of his joy. When he finished saying the final words *'Ayei Axmen!'*, the men began cheering and congratulating the boy. Ox lifted Obi onto his shoulders and danced in a circle like a wild horse. Even through the throbbing bruises of his beating, the boy's smile could not be contained. Ox dropped him to his feet and the captain and Bloody Son stuffed shavings of hashish into a highly-crafted bamboo water pipe. After siphoning a cloud of smoke from the conduit they offered it to the boy. Obi sucked the vapour from the draw pipe and threw up. He'd never tried a Jam Cap before. This only caused further rowdy screams of pleasure. Now, they were all high and Obi, staring into the thin brew of vomit and blood, ceased to feel his physical agony. Some of the psychoactive fumes had caused him to become euphoric. Soon he was laughing with the others. They fanned the bonfire with their hands like tribal dancers. Bloody Son perched himself on a small cluster of rocks by the shore and consecrated the new boy into office.

—You have passed your initiation. What do you wish to be?

Obi thought for only a second before blurting out.

—I wish to be a butcher! Just like Tom and Mephisto and every evil in the cosmos!

—Very well! You will now be referred to as Pigeon!

Obi didn't care that his nickname wasn't as impressive as his new friends. There would be time to earn his respect later.

4.

OBI RETURNED TO the university campus where Ogu was waiting for him. His arms embraced the boy with approval. Obi savoured the moment. He was officially a member of the family. The night before he had celebrated long into the early hours of the morning with Captain Cannibal, Ox, and Bloody Son. His eyelids weighed down with fatigue, dangling like a sack of Kobo coins. But he was fully awake once more.

—Pigeon, my new butcher!—cried Ogu triumphantly. He placed the Black Axe bandana around the boy's head and taught him the secret handshake of the group (Under, over, shake, snap, and slap). Obi couldn't help notice that the same flowered broche Asa once wore now slid up and down Ogu's forearm. The realisation that she had been seized of her beloved bracelet deflated Obi's soaring balloon of optimism.

Briefly he returned to his forgotten state of mind. He thought of his father, what he might make of all this. He'd say—Sometimes a father does all he can for his boy. Sometimes it doesn't feel like enough to the boy. Sometimes the boy feels the father has been really rather neglectful, in fact, but very rarely do fathers ever truly neglect their boy. How can a father not love his son and want to do everything within his power to see good by him? Exactly, it *can't* be the case, not ever.

It pleased Obi that he would soon be taught how to silence compassion completely. Currently, it stabbed him with a guilty nausea.

Children played outside the university gates. The only thing they had to fear in the near future was deciding diplomatically which games to play on that day. The Slave State hadn't consumed them yet, although they would inevitably be conscripted in the end. Obi saw a small boy gun down his friend with a toy gun. A little girl then kissed the gunmen on the cheek as if he was a hero and his prey was a mythical beast.

Obi knew he wasn't just a child with a toy gun. He knew his country wouldn't benefit from any of this. But it wasn't long before he returned to selfishness. To Ogu this entire fiasco seemed merely a part of the bloody theatre of life, to which he was in charge of its entire artistic direction. The boy needed to belong more than anything.

Ogu had called Pigeon into a circle with other Axe members. He was delivering plans for their next target.

—Aliyu, who leads "The Daughters of Jezebel", must be taken down. She prostitutes her members for money. Then uses that money to bribe teachers. As a result the female grades are better than the male. We must put a stop to this.

Obi was so wrapped up in Ogu's confident manner, the absurdity of his request didn't cross his mind.

—Pigeon, you, me, Ox, Panther, and Captain Cannibal will go. Panther, I need you for your pace. She'll try to run when she catches sight of me. Once she has been caught Ox and the captain will restrain her. I'll then rape her body while she's down, then Pigeon the Butcher will cut her head off from the neck. Here, pour this on her body to help it dissolve.

Ogu handed Pigeon a beaker of acid.

—Were going to work closer with Black Axe members from Obafemi Awalowo University in our attempts to completely eradicate the female confraternities forever. For too long we have allowed whores to behave like men.

His crowd cheered.

—We begin tomorrow at sundown! She'll be outside Yaba campus with the rest of her whores. But they won't give us much trouble!

That night Pigeon the Butcher practised chopping lumps out of a cottonwood tree. As the chunks of silky bark and sap yielded at the hands of his machete, Obi felt ready to accomplish his gruesome deed the following sundown. His thoughts were primarily of being seen in public with Ogu. Little time was spent preparing the execution, mentally or in technique. Obi was determined to complete his second murder without assistance.

By now, the boy was addicted to all kinds of counterfeit drugs that he believed to be real. Tonics for malaria shipped in from China or India seemed to possess a certain psychic charge that gave him the closest thing to an apathetic state of mind. When the Nigerian government decided to abandon the city long ago, a hoard of these pretend drugs found circulation among the Lagos marketplace. With the

Pharmaceutical Society of Nigeria distributing the pills from their base in the very city Obi occupied, getting your hands on a cheap high was easy. Only after consumption did Obi the Pigeon feel fully prepared.

The blood plasma which hammocks my lazy red cells
Sways, sways north bisecting the stoned soma
Disrupted alpha waves
The altered state of psycho-active conscious
—You can't . . .
—We can rearrange the stars to advertise in the sky. There is nothing we can't do.

In his transcendent state everything else seemed underwhelming. He experienced no sadness when walking through the garbage-filled streets of Lagos, or beholding the sight of five million struggling, corrupted fellow Nigerians. Their impoverishment was his gain. As far as he was concerned they were flesh and bone separated from him by divine right. He convinced himself it was ambition that gave him superiority, not just the Slave State. Obi fell asleep still wearing his bandana, clutching his weapon close to his heart.

The Black Axe all assumed family roles in Pigeon's head. Captain Cannibal was the strong older brother. Ox was the playful cousin. Bloody Son, the strict but protective uncle. And Ogu, the God, his mother, his lover.

Pigeon woke bright and early in his dorm room. Bloody Son, coincidently, lived just a few chambers down from his, so he wasn't surprised to find his hulking silhouette fill the frame of the entrance when he pulled open the door.

—Are you ready for tonight young one?—asked the looming lummox.

Obi replied—You bet I'm ready—then signalled to the hacked cottonwood outside his window.

—If you're sure—Bloody Son then returned to his room quietly.

As the sun began to hide itself behind the horizon, the boy's anxiety was growing. No matter how many drugs he took, his worry had started to manifest.

The journey over to the Yaba campus took longer than anticipated because of his sudden bout of stage fright. The stage floor seemed to last the full half mile walk, until he was finally presented with his audience. There was Ox pinning down the girl's left arm, judging him silently, his playfulness gone. Bloody Son held down the other arm and leered at Obi expectantly, unsure of the boy's ability as a warrior, almost hoping he might fail. Then there was Ogu tying his trouser belt back up, having just purged the girl of her dignity. He seemed to be the only Axe member whose eyes proved he had faith in the youngster. Aliyu screamed at the peak of her lungs, pouring sweat and tears over her captors. Her large brown lips rounded her mouth wide open, exhibiting a front set of immaculate teeth and deeper still, the emerging off-pink dimensions of a sandpapered tongue. This sight disturbed Obi. It didn't help that her skirt had been pulled to her ankles and was expected to stay there during and after her murder when the soul had left her body. This would be the final image people would have of her as she was placed perfectly in a ditch for some group of villagers to stumble across and mock.

This didn't *feel* right.

But now the moment of truth beckoned him to deliver a performance. He'd killed in the past—surely he could do it again? Hovering the machete above the girl, it was clear before long that he lacked the will. Hesitantly poising it, time and time again, pretending he was trying to make the perfect fatal cut. When minutes had passed and Pigeon the Butcher showed no signs of completing his task, Ogu swiped the blade from him and began chopping the girl up. Obi watched helplessly as Aliyu, stripped, exposed, beaten, and raped lost her distinctive physiognomy to her slaughterer's razor-sharp cleaver. Leaning over, allowing a thread of spit to fall from his lips, Ogu tipped the beaker of acid over what was left. Aliyu's body dissolved like a deforming ice sculpture coming into contact with a steaming hot Irish coffee. By the end the girl was unrecognisable as a human being. The massacre left both Obi and Ogu covered in a torrent of blood. Turning to face his idol, the boy feared the worst. However, all he was met by was a disappointed boy. Ogu's eyes looked forlorn by his new recruit's impudence instead of angry. In a way, this felt worse. Ogu handed the boy back his machete that was now swathed in viscera. Obi walked away, half expecting to be either called back and cast out of the Black Axe or attacked from behind by those who'd foolishly put faith in him. But they allowed him to leave.

Obi felt like he had no idea who he was anymore. The dark spirit, which had possessed him, appeared to be preparing to haunt a new host. If the boy couldn't belong to civil society or uncivil society, where did he belong?

He comforted himself by promising to redeem the next day by whatever means necessary.

5.

ON HIS WAY to school Obi saw a yellow school bus full of students seized by Nigerian militiamen. The driver was removed by the collar of his shirt and thrown from the vehicle into the street. After boarding the bus, armed officials told all the girls to get off with the driver before they opened fire on the remaining students, all young boys, all perhaps Inter-faith, before returning to their armoured cars and evacuating the area.

This didn't bring Pigeon the same satisfaction as the accident at Victoria Beach. Instead he worried that he may actually harbour some resentment towards the same government soldiers he was told he should respect and look up to. Again, guilty thoughts led his mind back to Asa, Kālu, and Aliyu. He cast his mind back to the fly.

Obi's schoolbag was now brimming with illegal items. He had replaced pencils with weapons and his packed lunch with cocktails of psychoactive drugs.

—Obi Bamgbala!—cried a familiar voice from behind him. He tossed his schoolbag into the locker then slammed it closed, before turning to see who had called after him. It was Mr. Abayomi. He was half leaning out of his classroom, beckoning the freshman over. Reluctantly Obi went over to him.

—Come in. Take a seat young man.

Obi remained standing defiantly.

—Or, you're welcome to stand of course. Would you mind if I asked you a few questions Obi?

—I don't have to answer anything.

—You're absolutely right. But would you perhaps humour me?

—Shoot old man.

—Why haven't you been in class the past week?

—I didn't want to go.

—Why? Don't you like my class?

—I don't like botany anymore. And I don't like you either—Obi felt instantly cold. Looking at its effect on Abayomi, the boy tried to retract.

—It's nothing personal. I don't like anyone.

—I've seen you, you know, with those boys.

—So?

—I'm concerned Obi! You aren't the boy I taught when you first arrived in my class.

—No. This *is* who I really am!

—No! It isn't . . . People are saying you killed Ucheoma Kālu. That's not you! Is this true?

—What's it to you?

—Obi please!

The boy grinned, but stayed silent.

—You're failing botany, boy. At this rate you won't get enough credits to take you into the next semester.

—I look like I care?

—Someone has implanted behaviour, an ideomotor reflex in you triggered by a word or phrase. You've just been responding to stimulus. I'm going to attempt to override this programme, but I need you to trust me. Let me show you this.

He trotted over to the collection of books in his

library case, picking one of the spines out with a spindly digit. Throwing open the binder, the professor flicked several pages until he found the chapter he wanted. He began to read aloud.

—The pineal gland. Essentially nothing more than a calcified region of the brain near the vicinity of the hypothalamus. Some claim it to be the source of all rationality and knowledge, and is said to allow an individual to see into the future when opened.

—So?

—So I want you to trust me for just a moment.

Abayomi placed both his thumb and forefinger on Obi's temples. The boy, staring into the old man's determined eyes. instantly demanded an explanation.

—What are you doing?

—Trust me. I'm opening your third eye, boy!

Abayomi reached over to Obi's head and prodded it in the centre hard. The boy could feel a barrier behind his skull begin to lift away as if a huge flood of knowledge was preparing to tip into his head. It stung and made his ears pop. Obi's nose began to bleed, and just as the third eye began to lift its lid, he pushed Abayomi away

—Don't touch me!

—Obi, I . . . I'm sorry! I just want you to *think*!

—You *will* let me pass botany old man!

—No, I will not.

—You will!—he became increasingly aggressive

—No. I will not. I cannot be bullied.

Obi pulled free his machete and severed the teacher's hand from its wrist. Abayomi went pale with shock as his dismembered hand lay a meter or so in front of him, jerking like a wrinkled live grenade ready to detonate. Blood squirted at a passionate rate from its stump. Abayomi's eyes and mouth fell open in disbelief. With his remaining hand the professor reached onto the table and retrieved something that he intended to give to his killer before the attack.

—Here. Take this—spluttered Abayomi, handing Obi a book of plays—*"The Trials of Brother Jero and The Strong Breed" by Wole Soyinka.*

—The last piece of literature allowed in this zone of the Slave State. You read that and you'll see—After scanning the cover for a second Obi lowered the hardback novel, revealing Abayomi's vacant stare. The old man was gone. Obi wept.

—*The reason I was unable to over-ride his hypnosis is because he used auto-suggestion on himself, no one implanted it there, he imposed this behaviour on himself!*

That night the moon was fat and full, raising the tides with its emission. Obi reflected from within his dorm room. Though the night was freezing cold, the very sight of the moon warmed the boy. Through all its familiar but remote canyons laden with minerals, the glowing body shone like a silver mirror, reflecting Obi's wrongs back onto the surface of the earth for all to see. He conversed with it in the silence of space. After smoking a Jam Cap Obi released himself of Earth's atmosphere and he found himself suddenly on the moon bed, sitting cross-legged and staring at its infinite black sky above, below and all around him. The moon was an individual—strange but wise. He was Nimrod and this was his Babel.

Obi opened the book of plays Abayomi gave him, starting first with *"The Trials of Brother Jero"*, which told the story of Jero, a charlatan prophet who gave all his sermons on the beach. In an attempt to dupe unsuspecting locals into becoming his disciples, the preacher sought to capitalise on the rise of Nigeria's widespread adoption of religious faith. "*The Strong Breed*", the second story, showed how the genuine healer, Eman, came to terms with his country's history of symbolic sacrifice. While giving free medical treatment and advice to the locals of a rural community, because was is a stranger, Eman was chosen as a carrier for the New Year's sacrifice that cleansed the village of sin. The boy saw. As Abayomi had promised, for the first time Obi saw. Comparisons between the selfish trickster Jero and Ogu were unmistakable. He felt ashamed.

Soft whispers all around him sympathised and promised him there was still time to change. Obi listened intently while staring hard at the lunar surface the colour of Dijon mustard. Looking down, the earth sighed back at him. When the beautiful female murmur had lulled the boy into sleep, Obi Bamgbala awoke, only now he was fully willing to let go of Pigeon for good. The moon was keen to keep the Butcher . . .

***

Pigeon stared down from the suicide barrier overlooking the
medical complex—students buzzed around the facility in
clusters. The air was still as dusk welted through the clear
sky. He climbed over the barrier and stood erect on the
ledge, the tips of his toes overhanging slightly. He began
to sway. He pushed his face into the oncoming breeze and
descended from the apex in a starfish formation towards the
tarmac below . . .

TRUTH

THE BLACK AXE headquarters weren't really based within the university. Obi discovered the truth soon. Captain Cannibal arranged to meet the boy to show him the true location of the group as well as the origins of its leader.

—Boy, you do not seem certain of your place here.—boomed the captain as he led Obi away from the campus enclave.—You lack the will to kill for what you believe in. Only once I have shown you the truth will you have proved your devotion.

—Come Pigeon—he demanded, but the boy was hesitant to respond to this title anymore. Obi still carried the heavy burden of guilt.

The two travelled deep into the heart of Lagos. Scammers opened their long trench coats to reveal numerous knock-off purchases for sale, but the captain barely blinked an eyelid. Obi did not speak a word. A black dog free of its leash had suddenly wrapped itself around the boy's leg. Obi found it difficult to muster enough anger to smite the animal that had mistaken his shin for a bitch. But after he became aware of the captain's doubtful glare looming over him, Obi lifted his leg free and kicked the stray away. The black dog's stench stayed with him.

Now at a dark narrow alleyway, Captain Cannibal gestured to the boy that they were almost at their destination. Obi looked back through the crack that showed the city fully and glimpsed young children carrying granite blocks on their heads from stall to stall at Oshodi marketplace. Moleu buses vomited black clouds of greenhouse gas that rested on layers of burning biomass, hovering above the city ominously. For the first time in a while, it affected him greatly.

Obi was presented on the other side of the alley by a small grey building block with weathered concrete walls. Surrounding it was a cast iron fence that protected the modest fortress within. Above, the clouds stuck together in the shapes of two albino horses and a swelling bald eagle. The weather soon changed. Bolts of lightning cut through the clouds, dispersing the misty remains of the fogged animals across the canvas of the sky as a bank of rain teamed from their exposed wounds. Obi lifted up the hood of his jacket.

—This is it boy—admitted the captain who used the cape of his anorak for shelter.

On the gates, two traversing axe blades displayed the movement's crest. Spray painted across the emblem was "Blackism is real. You wouldn't understand."

Captain Cannibal explained that a rival gang had covered the entire headquarters in graffiti as an instigation of war.

The two armed policemen guarding the premises were built broad like huge mechanical soldiers. One had a row of broken teeth like piano keys. The other never blinked. However, they both allowed the captain and the boy to enter.

Cutting odours of sex and alcohol moistened the inner recesses of the clubhouse. The boy choked on the dirty oxygen filling the hallway. Obi stuck close to the captain as he ventured up several flights of stairs; past comatose policemen with white powder smudged over their nose and mouth; past hookers being beaten and abused; past laughing figures playing poker, swearing and looking suspiciously important in their suites. When the final set of stairs had been defeated, the captain signalled to the boy that they had reached the end. The boy was led through a set of teak bamboo-beaded door curtains. Inside, a golden cauldron bubbled and filled the chamber with steam. From the walls hung pots, tarps, and weapons. Resting on a mantelpiece were precious Faberge eggs above an ottoman upholstered in jewels.

Obi saw something that shocked him instantly.

Ogu was bowing, bowing on his knees to a small man draped in a loose-fitting buba blouse and a filla head cap; the small man sported several overweight crowned heads on his knuckles. Ogu kept calling him "*Doctor Chopin*".

Obi was clenched with fear. The doctor was surrounded by minders and fully-armed policemen. His fortress was bathed in a thick smoky chaos of cigarette fumes. Through the vapour Ogu stuck out like a sore thumb, utterly humbled by this mere mortal. The captain waited by the door until Doctor Chopin was ready to see him.

Obi couldn't help notice how pathetic his idol seemed. Despite having let go of Pigeon, it took this image of Ogu kissing someone else's charms to completely bring an end to his doubts. Chopin seemed to be in charge of everything the Black Axe were responsible for. Swiftly, the doctor pushed Ogu's head away and advanced towards Obi and the captain.

—Cannibal! Who is this?

—This is Pigeon sir.

—*Sir?*—thought Obi, confused by the power this one individual owned over more physically intimidating figures.

—Pigeon? The coward I've been hearing about?— he said dryly.

Obi lowered his head, hiding as far behind his hood as he could. Then Ogu stood and pointed accusingly.

—Yes sir that's him.

Obi was disgusted by the boy he once held in such high regard. To Obi, it was Ogu who was the real coward. Dr. Chopin was still reprimanding Pigeon.

—I know you boy . . . I recognise your stench.

Obi's face was a portrait of guilt and fear.

—Oh, dear oh dear. This is unfortunate. You have not only disgraced the Black Axe small one, but you have disrespected your superiors and now you must be discharged.

Chopin's eyes were like two brown dishes staring through the boy. As Obi had dreaded, he had been led into a trap to punish him for his unwillingness to kill. The doctor tore free Obi's headscarf, tossing it behind him. Now stripped of his membership, the captain stood aside, allowing the doctor some space to approach further. The room, with its half-naked woman and army men, was almost like a gangster's brothel. Chopin clicked his fingers and two guards jumped to their feet to tend his needs.

—Take the boy to the roof of Lagos University and teach him a lesson he won't soon forget. Ogu, you conduct proceedings. I want a swift but educational operation. Go.

Obi now found himself being raised by his armpits into the air then backwards through the beaded door by the soldiers. Cannibal joined a brunette dancer on the couch, stirring the fatty witch's brew of the cauldron with his finger.

Obi was dragged through the narrow alleyway rearwards and back into the bustling metropolis of Lagos city centre. Oshodi Marketplace cleared a divide so the army men could shepherd their prisoner through the chaos of commerce. The two soldiers ushering him violently into civilisation looked only forward, but behind them, in front of the boy, tramped Ogu. He smirked dimly, half intoxicated, blithe to his betrayal.

***

Obi knew he was near the university. All the people around him watched on, unconcerned by the soldiers who escorted the boy to the roof of the building. Ogu said nothing the whole journey. His facial expression remained stationary in the same casual smirk for several minutes. There was something even more terrifying in Ogu's absent stare.

Obi's shoes slipped off and the orange sand of the gravel football pitch burned the soles of his bare feet. Ogu's pleasure was noticeably tweaked by the sight of the freshman's agony. Eventually he mouthed, *"I'll swallow your soul . . . "* but Obi wasn't taken aback.

The boy *hated* Ogu now.

On campus the university day was just ending, so the evacuating hoard of students left class just in time to witness whatever was about to happen to Obi Bamgbala. Teachers locked up their classrooms and came outside to the playing field to see what was attracting the students.

Greg Chima, Professor Abayomi's replacement, saw Obi Bamgbala being prepared for execution. Rushing to the window, Chima dialled the principle but could get no answer. He abandoned his mountain of jotters and un-graded essays to join the rest of the campus population on the ivory tower arena.

Some students seemed to relish the thought of seeing an execution, turning up a storm of palm wine music from their boom boxes and cheering. Others, including Greg Chima, despaired helplessly.

Obi was carted over one of the soldier's shoulders like a sack of potatoes. The landing hallway was a cold grey steel. Each step conquered was another stride towards his imminent demise. Their footsteps echoed in the empty hollowness of the reinforced passage. Ogu slowly lumbered behind the soldiers, still smirking emptily. Obi still wasn't sure of his past idol's true power. Even after his submission to Doctor Chopin, the boy still looked inherently evil. There was still a presence which surrounded him.

At the crown of the staircase, a metal door to the top garret was barged open by one of the men. Strong, sudden jets of air filled Obi's lungs as the light of outside space blinded him. With a careless thud the soldiers unloaded Obi.

The boy's trousers were removed, then the rest of his clothes until all he had left was his underpants to conceal his shame. Ogu supervised with a perverse concentration. He nodded and the soldiers took a step back. The evil Ogu backed his naked prey onto the edge of the building. Beneath, forty feet below, a baying populace of students anticipated Obi Bamgbala's fall to the hard floor of concrete.

JUMP!—Yelled one boy only to be clouted behind the ear by a bemused professor Chima. Two visiting Slave State missionaries were shocked by the events taking place but did nothing to prevent it.

Ogu moved closer. Obi sweated nervously, both by his nakedness and how close he was to the edge. Some girls wolf-whistled up at him. The boy could not control his embarrassment. Chima tried dialling the police from his cellphone but abandoned the idea when he caught sight of the militia men on top of the building helping Ogu. Obi had lost, then regained his purpose in lifeX—now, it was disappearing once more.

He contemplated jumping. Just like Abayomi, Asa, Kālu and Aliyu, no one would care if he died tonight or not. His father was miles away. His mother was long gone, pursuing a job as a canoeist for tourists in Onitsha. She left shortly after Obi was born. As Ogu sneaked closer, Obi snubbed the easy escape offered by the key holder to the kingdom of unconsciousness, choosing instead to fight for the privilege of life.

Obi, lunging forward like a vicious cat spreading its paws and presenting its knives, managed to back himself out of the corner. Ogu was chanting again. His eyeballs spun to the back of his head as his grin widened.

Professor Chima was growing impatient, and was growing tired too, of being bullied into submission by corrupt authority. The missionaries watched as

Chima ran into the front door of the building, gasping at the courage they did not possess. Groups of students continued cheering, but were disappointed that Obi had escaped his position near the edge.

Back on the rooftop, Ogu had retrieved the beaded wand from his belt and was nearing the end of a spell. All the boy could do now was charge. Both militiamen looked decidedly unfazed by the art of "*juju*".

Chima struggled to seize a breath as he loped up each step. He was motivated by a desire to save an innocent life. Greg Chima did not know that Obi Bamgbala was not such an innocent life.

At the foot of the stairs, the main door which led onto the roof was locked. Chima tried yelling, then barging with his shoulder. The teacher had very little energy left after climbing the stairs, and the door would not budge. Chima noticed a hole in the brickwork where the fire escape used to be. It was now covered in palm leafs and flourished with plant life. He wasted no time climbing onto the ledge. The undergrowth was thick and lush after being used by botany students as a test area for growing shrubs. Chima crept to the side of the building where a ladder hinged along a track would take him to the roof.

The only problem facing Obi was that he was unarmed and naked. Ogu's fingers were outstretched antennas dredging through the summer air, wiggling and teasing like eight long cylinders of dark magic. His eyes were still blank white, save the odd blossoming of viscera.

Obi took his chance.

Pouncing with his left foot in front of him, he sent his hands around Ogu's throat. His former idol choked and ceased his ritualistic chant.

Chima pulled himself along the ledge of the New Lagos science dept window and up onto the top garret. His presence had been made known. While one soldier tried to help Ogu free him of his attacker, the other noticed Chima's arrival and bounded towards him.

—Stop! You are under arrest!—warned the soldier, but the professor did not stop. The soldier pulled free his pistol and fired once into the air, then concentrated the gun's aim in the direction of the intruder.

Obi was now on the ground. Ogu rubbed the area of his neck which had been throttled. The crowd below grew impatient. They demanded blood.

Having landed fiercely on the concrete, the boy hadn't even heard the two gunshots. It was only when Ogu began laughing maniacally that Greg Chima's corpse, silent and wilted into a ball like an unopened flower, was realised. The soldier who had shot him approached unperturbed.

—We don't have time for this. Kill the boy quickly so we can get out of here.

His colleague nodded in agreement. However, Ogu was adamant on personal retribution.

—Come boy. Do your thing or I'll shoot him right here, right now - threatened the more robust of the two soldiers. Ogu did not answer.

—Boy! Do as I say—His voice boomed.

The crowd below took a step back at the rumbling thunder of his demand like some angry voice from Heaven. Finally, Ogu resigned himself to the colossal warrior's order. He walked up to Obi almost dreamily uninterested. Lightly, he dusted off the boy's naked shoulders for him. He placed both palms on either side of Obi's chest, before thrusting them into his body and sending the freshman over the side of the university building.

Obi looked up as he flew backwards, preparing to be obliterated by the solid asphalt strip. Time decelerated. Above him the clouds dispersed. However, his whole life somehow failed to flash before him as he'd anticipated; broadening his arms out like a glorious martyred angel gave the boy one last instant of clarity. He could hear the soldiers celebrate, grateful for Ogu's eventual co-operation. He could see Ogu watching as his body fell, enthusiastically waiting for the big bloody finish. He sensed the crowd clear a grave for him. Obi landed.

CRUCIFIXION

THE BOY'S TOMB, while wide and willing, did not succeed in burying Obi Bamgbala. He dreamed, but his sleep was far from eternal. He dreamed of a faceless man being mounted onto a large wooden crucifix. His sweat was as blood. Battered, exhausted, and dehydrated, the man was scourged relentlessly by a long leather whip. Tentacled throngs descended onto his bare shoulders and back, blowing open deep wounds under repeated lashings. An unrecognisable bulk of bleeding skin and tissue cried an agonised wail. Two rusty nails bore deep into the frail bone of his wrist while another two nails pinned the metatarsal in his ankles and feet, fastening him to the crucifix. The man was then untied. Obi saw him wet with his own blood, unable to stand up. Slumped on the asphalt. Crowds of people stoned him to death. There was no mercy. And then Obi woke up.

Standing over him was a doctor wearing a surgeon mask. As he walked in and out of the boy's view, Obi saw his own leg bandaged up, cast in a sling and strung up on a hoist. He quailed in agony, but could only raise his head fractionally out of a stationery position. The doctor came back, this time without his visor.

—You're very lucky. Two missionaries carried you all the way to the infirmary. That was quite a fall.

Obi tried to talk but choked.

—Don't speak son. Just rest. You've broken both your legs and your shoulder. There's a neck sprain in there too. Any next of kin will be notified as soon as possible.

The doctor left, examining his clipboard closely.

A young girl looked on with a stretched face of illness. It was suspected some kind of yellow fever had torn through her system. Doctors later diagnosed the girl as suffering from the Black Dog. She gazed at Obi absent-mindedly as though she were scrutinizing deep beneath the seams of his soul. Her eyes begged for mercy, for something comforting. Obi could ignore her no longer. He sensed the girl's eyes upon him.

—I'm Obi. What's your name?—he began, clearing his throat.

—N'gozi. It means "blessing"—replied the girl without delay.

The girl was a streetwalker, Obi could tell. She was twelve or thirteen and provocatively dressed. Above her lip, puffing outwards with damaged tissue, was a large bruise. Using what she had to get what she needed. It became clear also that N'gozi was pregnant. The boy wondered if this was how she'd contracted the disease—working on the street. Either way she would never be allowed to keep her child. She was a child herself.

Sending a brittle arm over to Obi's bed-sit, she studied his cast. Her muscles were wasted by the virus, which was slowly dismantling her body's immune system.

—What's your baby's name?

—If it's a boy "Daniel", and "Anne" if it's a girl.

N'gozi spoke as if her child were a doll for playing with. Obi smiled stiffly.

—What are you in for?—Obi asked, as if he didn't know. A searing current of pain surfed along his neck as he tried to see N'gozi.

—My mother left my father for Lagos a few years ago. An aunt of mine told me she knew where she was. She took me to the city and promised my mother would be waiting. But my mother wasn't there. My aunt told me I would work in the slaughterhouse as a hooker to pay for her home instead.

—Did a man hit you there?

—No. Her husband is an evil man. He impregnated me. My aunt is infected. My cousins had been infected by her breast milk. They spat at me. Now I'm ill.

Obi thought less about his own selfish pain.

—I'm sorry N'gozi.

The girl crossed her legs on the bed, swaying back and forth, rather pleased to have gained her neighbour's sympathy.

—That's okay. Why are you here then?

—*There would be no harm in telling a dying girl the truth of my sins?*—thought Obi in a somewhat triumphant return to his original selfishness. The truth was eating the boy up from the inside. Like a potent, highly toxic virus which attacked the heart and soul, Obi had to admit all before his transgressions could be fully absolved.

Obi started with his arrival in New Lagos city, and finished the story with him lying in that very hospital bed. As predicted, the boy felt suitably relieved of his burden. His injuries throbbed less. Even so, N'gozi, while nodding intently, couldn't hide that her awareness was drifting in the after effects of poor health. She stifled numerous yawns to be polite but it was obvious she didn't have long. The brownness of her cheeks ran paler with ruined blood. N'gozi had drunk her unreasonably short fountain dry. And still she listened to the boy's story, determined to mask her weariness. By the end of Obi's accounts, N'gozi found that, even as exhaustion threatened to prevail, that her opinion on her neighbour was not a negative one.

—Do you think I'm a bad person?—he eventually pleaded.

Now being swept away from the living, N'gozi uttered—

—No Obi. You don't have the viscera eyes.

The girl and her unborn child closed their eyes gently. Then they were gone.

Obi could not see her die but sensed both souls leave the room. The girl had died alone with no family by her side. Obi wondered if her mother knew that her sister had caused her daughter's death. Obi wondered if N'gozi's mother would care. There was something unpoetic about her dying and his continuation. He felt guilty again. Minutes later he saw paramedics and doctors hurry past his bed. Obi heard the main nurse cry. A time of death was issued before her under covers were placed over her body. N'gozi was then wheeled away to the morgue. There, her child (*Daniel/Anne*) would be cut from her stomach having never breathed a drop of air into its lungs.

Obi realised something. Maybe *he* was alive for a reason. Right now, it was difficult to determine what his purpose could be, but he was filled with a new sense of himself.

6.

OVER THE COMING months, Obi regained the use of his arms and worked his way back to fitness. Often he would think of N'gozi. He started writing a letter to his father in Okpella. It read—

> *Dear father,*
>
> *Lagos is a big city. I miss Okpella and the farm. I hope you won't be angry or disappointed but I have left university. Hopefully I'll see you soon to explain. I hope you're keeping well. I miss you very much. I promise I'll find a way to make you proud of your son again.*
>
> *Love*
> *Obi*

And so the boy sought to exorcise himself of his afflictions. Obi glowed in the presence of the city's lights. Daytime brought a beautiful luminosity. All at once the bright chutes poured in, N'gozi navigating them in his direction. Of course, with the good, there were equal measures of the bad. Sometimes there would be rain and bleakness. Sometimes N'gozi's pardoning words seemed nothing more than the morphine-prompted slackening of a dying girl's jaw. Asa, Kālu, and Aliyu would visit him to deliver disturbing truths about the pain of dying. When the ghosts came, Obi buried his head inside a pillow until they disappeared with the parting black clouds. Chima came to look at the boy responsible for killing him. Obi hadn't felt it was his fault, but then Abayomi would shuffle from the dark corner of the room to remind him of his blame. Abayomi presented the most unpleasant phantom. When he materialized, Obi rarely spoke. When the professor called him *"Murderer"*, *"Judus"* or condemn accusingly that he was "A *disappointment*", the boy never gave a reply.

The nurse brought Obi a plate of food. He picked at it with a plastic fork. N'gozi had a boy—Daniel was its name. He knew because it had suddenly started showing up at night when Obi was preparing for sleep. At the end of a good day he'd appear. A happy day would never have a happy night. Almost as if young, unborn Daniel had to remind Obi Bamgbala that he wasn't ready to live a life free of guilt just yet. Daniel, while undeveloped, represented what should have been. N'gozi *should* have had a richer existence. She *should* have nursed a rag doll bought for her by doting parents, rather than harbouring the foetus of a doomed bastard child. Her adult life *should* have been simple but full, deserving of all things good. Daniel was the silent, ghostly reminder that the Slave State was everywhere. If the universe no longer felt someone merited life, then it would tear it away in a blinking instant. It had grown tired of young, innocent N'gozi. Obi would have to do a lot to prove he earned his breath.

In the infirmary Obi's room was beginning to look more and more like purgatory. N'gozi's bed remained empty. No one would occupy that bed again. He hadn't seen a doctor in what felt like weeks. The fruit bowl beside him rotted away to degraded soft mass. On all sides of him, the hospital chamber felt like a prison cell. Its walls contracted, creeping narrower, boxing him in. Soon, Obi felt, he would be squashed like a sardine in a tin. There hadn't been any traces of light for days.

Obi only hoped he was being purified in preparation for Heaven. He hoped he was hallucinating. Panic struck as he realised there was no one else in the room. N'gozi smiled deeply, half covered in shadow. While thoughtful looking, there was something nightmarish about her.

—Please—Obi cried—I don't want to be the Butcher anymore. Please leave me alone . . .

The girl kept smiling, unruffled. From the blackness of the sheltering shadow, N'gozi brought Daniel into the light, cradling him softly. His face embalmed in oily rags.

—Why do you haunt me? I want to die in Un's friendship. Please!

—Un? Obi, you are one of the grossly mislead. Forget about mortal sins and cleansing fire because what you're experiencing is something much more . . . —N'gozi struggled to find the word she wanted— Much more . . . —The sentence lingered uncompleted until Abayomi came forth, submitting his guidance— . . . much more tangible.

He spoke dryly, placing his one undamaged hand on the girl's shoulder.

—What am I experiencing?—wept the broken boy who gushed an intense waterway of tears.

—Do not cry. Your soul has come as close to death as it will for years. You forgot who you were, boy.

—Only those of strong mindedness can overcome temptations of the vice. You are the folly, I am the death.

—What do I have to do to save myself?

—Admitting your transgressions is not enough. Feeling a glimmer of guilt is not enough. Crying in the direction of visiting ghosts from your past will not be enough either. Slave State society will fail to punish you. Though there is no God or Heaven or Hell, you must be punished to save humanity. Look into my eyes. Look into this girl's eyes. We will never leave you. Till the day you die, we will never leave you. The most effective punishment is done by the self in the prison of the mind.

Death was leaving. When the hospital room began brightening up again, life seemed to re-appear from the immense black cape of the reaper. For now at least, the fruit in the bowl was round and seasoned. Doctors and nurses started to emerge from the halls into intensive care wards. Some wheeled carts of IV drips and dialysis equipment to patients who no longer looked like ghosts. Reality had returned. Rain descended from the parted clouds, drumming against the window ledge like the sounds of a furious locomotive.

He learned to walk with the aid of a mental health nurse. It took only three days until his knees were strong enough to support his thighs. Obi knew he had to return home.

THE HOLINESS OF HOME

OBI DIDN'T BOTHER discharging himself from university the proper way. Too many forms. Too much hassle. It wasted too much time, time that he felt he was short of. It also ran the risk of crossing Ogu or the Black Axe again. If they knew he was alive they would finish the job there and then. University would not be missed. All his belongings locked away in his dorm room were things he did not need. Obi was keen to leave the disgrace of his New Lagos University experience behind for good.

As the rapid transport bus pulled into its terminal, relief swept over him. The chariot had arrived. He would be taken straight along the Benin highway to Edo state. On board the bus, Obi threw his empty food cartons under the seat before dropping himself heftily onto the window side. He strained with vague memories of his mother. Soon the driver brought the automatic door closed, un-creasing flat out from its half sail. Obi's mother was taller than most woman. She was young, only nineteen when his father impregnated her. Obi remembered the silky whisper of her nightgown as she cradled him in his cot. He remembered arguing. Soft organs leaking from eye-hole cavities.

The bus engine revved and rumbled into life. Backing out of the depot, he was well on his way to freedom. One minute she was there, the next she was gone. Obi believed her to have been beautiful. His father told him on many occasions his mother was the toast of Okpella, that even the State wouldn't send her to an enclave. He sensed that his mother had hurt his father greatly by leaving. Perhaps not as saddened as he would be if he ever discovered his son's behaviour.

Lost in his work, ensuring the farm thrived, this was his new lover. Obi knew that he was lucky not to have known her or he would have shared a similar torture with his father. The boy slipped into a slumber. He dreamt of nothing.

When Obi awoke, he was entering Okene-Abuja federal highway. The familiarity of Okpella loosened him up. It would not be long until the bus would pass Utayoke Primary School.

In the station, Obi remained seated for a few minutes after the bus came to a stop. He thought about what he would tell his father. He wondered if he could ever forgive him. More importantly, Obi wondered if he could ever forgive himself. Asa came into his mind. She was such a unique, delicate creature. When she showed him undue kindness in the beginning, she had been compelling even then. When she kissed Wilson, Obi felt waves of resentment stronger than anything he'd felt before. As she mourned the death of Wilson, Asa had appeared more brittle but retained something inwardly strong and alluring. Obi had never been so attracted to a woman like that before. It felt as if it had been a different person brainwashed by the Black Axe. But it was he. It was he who led the unsuspecting, grieving girl into the hands of a murderous cult. What had happened to him at university?

—Hey! You in the back! This bus stops here. Off!— the driver hollered at Obi, fixing his driving cap and looking as eager faced to leave the vehicle as a petulant child desperate for privacy. Eventually the boy stood up and disembarked along the deep meandering curves of the coach corridor. Obi did not share a glance with the leering driver.

Obi was a virgin. He was what his father called "a late developer". His hair was cropped but un-styled. Eczema wreaked havoc on his under ears, pillaging his brow and forearms. He wore elbow length t-shirts with pictures of smiling faces or tropical palm tree silhouettes on them. His eyes were childlike, big and unassuming. In Okpella he fit in because it was such a small town. New Lagos found him out straight away. Exposed him as immature. Unready. Obi realised that Lagos demonstrated how he had grown up quick but chosen the wrong route. This was something he had to live with. The Black Axe lured him too easily. Obi worried he might've been seen as stupid instead of barbaric. If truth be told, Obi just wanted to belong to something. With his father miles away in a different state the boy longed for guidance. He was prepared that no one would understand this. It didn't excuse his actions.

As soon as Obi had arrived in the marketplace his mood changed. He felt at home once more, settled. His heart never really left. Every stall was neatly arranged, full of healthy foods sold by friendly people he recognised. Not like Lagos. His auntie's friend Laila waved from behind her stands of maize and lentil. Her wide smile, affectionately remembering

Obi's face, was something which almost reduced the boy to tears.

Obi tasted an apple offered to him by a vendor.

—A bit under ripe—Obi confessed.

—It's the season. You should stock up before there's none left.

—No fruit?

—Most farms had their stock destroyed by the oil.

—The oil?

—A ruptured pipeline spilled gallons of crude oil onto Okpella. Didn't you hear?

—But my father owns a farm in Okpella!

—Not anymore he doesn't. What's your father's name?

—Kayode Bamgbala.

—Bamgbala? You're Bamgbala's son?

—Yes why?

—Come through the back. There's something I must tell you.

Obi followed the vendor behind his stall. His stomach was clenched in a tight ball.

—I knew your father. He was a good man. A hard-working man. That is why it difficult to tell you this information.

—What is it?

—The oil spill contaminated our drinking wells. Your father drank some of the polluted water. He died of dysentery. I'm sorry.

＊

Obi travelled to his father's old farm. It was worse than he'd imagined. A line of dead goats lay on the burned grass. Sure enough, an old well overflowed with thick crude oil, flowing into the reservoir which led into town. Obi felt his anger return and felt the utter futility in striving to be good . . .

His eyes burned. Parabolic mirrors ran red, vestigial organs reawaken, head throbs with enough anger and fire to turn a migraine into Transmatica . . .

Blowtorched eyes, brilliant sequins sewn on a shroud, angles of light dancing in the diaphragm . . .

BIRTH, SEX, DEATH, STIGMATA

LIZZY STRIDE . . .

. . . and then she became the first woman. Regenerated from basic cells, stardust and clay, she was a miracle of beauty, a template mould hidden behind a burka and oppressive Djeballa. Her mouth silenced by a veil. She had been born then instantly hidden and shame was her first definable emotion.

Men in reed hats still saw fit to leer from stalls, their faces stuffed like geese—or at least they *looked* like men upon first glance. Closer observations would reveal their true heritage. 'The Broods' they were called, extants of the original epoch. They were apelike creatures who roamed the desert pavements and dunes in travelling kiosks. They became gibbering atrocities in the presence of virginal perfume.

Lizzy walked through the ancient city still swathed in amniotic latex. Her bare toes wriggled through leather slippers and the Broods lifted from their stools and leaned in. She did not yet know her body but was aware of the pulse between her thighs. The entire Kasbah became aware of it too.

An aboriginal-looking vendor called Druitt

appeared and began prattling in a primitive tongue. He was gesturing to a southerly protuberance. Lizzy followed his long, wart-thrown fingers and met the winking, weeping eye of his cock. This was the first time she had seen a cock. It coiled ever upwards in her presence; Druitt wanted to impale her with it. Slowly he moved towards Lizzy. He reached for her orange shawl and tugged it free of her shoulders.

—You fuck dogs, so you can fuck *this*?—Druitt said in passing indictment.

He tugged at the scarlet ball at the end of his shaft and leered.

—I don't fuck dogs—Lizzy hated that these were the first words she ever released into the air. She wanted to stuff them back into her mouth.

—You fuck dogs. You have long hair and strange unnatural swellings and a smell of poverty about you... the kind who can afford to fuck only dogs.

—I . . .

—Touch it . . .

Lizzy obediently motioned her hand towards the cock. The arid planes were ghostly silent, viscera eyes watched without blinking.

—I have to fill you full of this fluid see, to fill the half-deflated doll of your body; the only thing that could breathe life and fullness into your wrinkled, comatose husk is my spermatic solution.

An inch from Druitt's cock, the report of a rifle halted everything in its tracks . . .

A figure on a camel stood in the far reaches of a rock outcrop, a caravan of nomads trailing behind him with their flock. They came down to the city, The Broods glared hatefully as they made their way past the cordon of boulders. The men looked human. The figure with the rifle looked very human in fact, as did his followers. Druitt began furiously masturbating, swearing under his breath. He gushed forth a kind of ejaculation as protest. The group of men approached Lizzy.

—Druitt doesn't know what he's doing, and neither do you. He doesn't know shit from shinola, a sad student of impotent Ostrog's teachings.

Druitt collapsed on a sand hill, exhausted and irritable.

—Fuck you paleface scum . . .

—My name is Cutbush. These are my partners, Deeming and Sadler.

Two of the nomads appeared on either side of Cutbush's camel. Deeming was naked and his hands were cuffed, although he was clearly not a slave—certainly not a kept slave. Sadler was a tall man of about six foot seven with tan complexion and wiry hair on his chest and chin. The bunched biceps of his arms were a pale bronze. Cutbush himself was simian in appearance but was not of the Brood.

—We'd like you to come join our buggering party. Our world is a place of guns and rape and humanity. Leave these animals and copulate with your own.

His primate face grinned. Lizzy climbed atop Cutbush's camel and locked her arms around his waist.

They about turned and left the city of masturbating monsters.

The moon quartered the sky. They had been travelling for hours on end. Eventually a gruff voice emerged from Cutbush.

—Do you have a name?

—I was given a name . . .

—Yes, and what is it?

—It's not a common name, at least I don't think it's common in this world.

Cutbush gave a belly laugh. Lizzy felt the muscles in his stomach contract in a pack of six.

—Not common in this world? Were you born only yesterday?

—This morning, I believe.

—You are the fattest baby I've ever seen.

Lizzy looked off into the distant verticals of the nomad city.

—I can feel your pulse, smell your desire. When we get to the city I will relieve you, then my lovers will relieve you.

—I've never . . . that's to say, I haven't . . . ever . . .

Cutbush yanked on the reign and his camel stopped. The shadowing nomads stopped too.

—You have never . . . copulated?

Lizzy said nothing. She didn't understand why, but she felt a great humiliation tugging at her every sinew.

—You have never even touched your own cock?

Lizzy knew she couldn't answer this. She didn't have a cock, not like Druitt's anyway. Cutbush dismounted his camel and then jerked Lizzy down from the saddle.

—Remove your robes!—Cutbush was furious. Lizzy's confusion and embarrassment had stolen her tongue. The great simian took one sharp step forward and tore open Lizzy's garments at the crotch. The nomads gasped in harmony.

—It has... nothing!

They all stared at the girl's smooth, sparsely pricked genitals.

—How is this possible?

—I don't know . . . I haven't had enough time to understand it myself—the girl tried to explain. The lumbering presence of Sadler appeared.

—It's not so unusual, Gull and Sickert . . .

—Gull and Sickert were castrated for insubordination!—Cutbush interrupted.

—Isn't it entirely plausible that this one has also been cut in a similar way?

—I wasn't cut—Lizzy protested. Becoming increasingly impatient, Cutbush knelt to her exposed genitals, placed two heavy hands on her thighs and nuzzled. Lizzy squirmed uncomfortably at first then surprised even herself when she reached out to clutch Cutbush's head and pushed his tongue deeper. He lapped back and forth and the nomad posse stood watching with utter shock as the girl moaned. Cutbush pulled his head away and spat on the ridges of sand.

—What *are* you??—he demanded, licking the lead of his wrist band, preferring the sand-blasted metal taste to Lizzy's own natural juices.

—You weren't created by the replicating machine were you?—Sadler asked, helping Cutbush to his feet.

—That makes it one of the Brood?

—No, I was conceived by the cosmos—Lizzy insisted.

—Ha! It's a god all of a sudden.

Sadler stood before the girl. He studied her naked front and sighed.

—There are no lacerations. It's as if it were *born* without a cock, like some freak of nature, an abomination . . .

Lizzy's head bowed. She was as innocent as any

newborn and yet was judged with such hateful abandon. Sadler saw the pain in her face and the feminine spirit in him that lingered in the recesses of his heart came to surface.

—I suppose . . . even if it is a freak of nature, it is not entirely its fault.

—Not its fault? What is this? It doesn't . . .

—Sir, please, we can't presume to know *anything* about it—Sadler turned to Lizzy and addressed her.

—You say you were born this morning, a child of the cosmos? Well we are children of the Replicator. We are clones. Although we claim to despise the Brood, we are inexorably linked to them. We are their descendants, the next stage . . . if you come to our city we will show you.

Cutbush reluctantly allowed Sadler to speak outside his authority because he was undeniably fascinated by Lizzy Stride.

***

That night they camped on the ergs. Sadler and Cutbush were engaging in anal sex—Sadler's giant frame dominated the comparatively small stature of his leader. Lizzy considered her birth, her death, and its inevitability; she had no idea about the bit in between.

Deeming was sitting cross-legged, his chained hands resting on his knees. He watched Lizzy with a patient lust. His eyes, first like glittering Chrysolite, then like poisonous green liquid, congealed in two hard marbles.

—*I'll get you*—he mouthed. The girl tried to ignore his threats.

She saw a lion withered to nothing in the mosaic of smooth stones and sand, its ribcage visibly trembling. She lay down, invited the lion to feed from her flesh and muscle and bone. The lion etched closer, either baffled by the gesture or distrusting of the act itself. It dually fed from her. Lizzy died clutching a stem of grapes.

She would be re-born the next day.

***

The city was magnificent—the buildings were set in tessellated tiles, giant stone phalli's stuck out of the sand and the front gates were mortared with semen, sweat, and wadded sputum. Lizzy held her breath when they entered through the gates. She was now walking beside Sadler and Deeming. Cutbush continued to lead the line.

They approached a polished, titanium structure which jutted out of the sediment like a giant machine-cock. Cutbush got off his camel and waited for the others to catch up. He halted Sadler.

—Are you sure about this? We can't go around exposing our genesis to just any old freak, especially a freak without a fucking cock!

—Sir, perhaps if we can study the abomination we can learn *more* about where we came from.

Cutbush nodded grudgingly, lowered his halting hand.

—Ok, let's . . .

Cutbush and Sadler were alerted to the sudden sound of a woman's screams. They ran to its source and saw Deeming on top of Lizzy. His cuffed wrists were joined around her throat and he had mounted her from behind. He was yelling like a maniac.

—Jesus! Look at the blood! Christ! Look at this blood, I think I'm killing her!

Sadler dived at Deeming, pulling his blood-swathed cock free of the girl. She lay quivering with her cheek against the sand. All she could think about was the pain; she had felt less pain while being mauled by the lion.

Sadler drew back a fist and smashed his giant, serrated knuckles into Deeming's mouth so hard that a scatter of teeth came flying out.

—Why are oo punfing me??—Deeming begged, choking on a round of his own bloody saliva.

—WHY? WHY?? WHY AM I PUNCHING YOU?

He drove another fist into Deeming's pulped face again and again until the skull completely caved in and Sadler was left laying into a wet bag of bones.

—ENOUGH!—Cutbush ordered. Sadler ceased his furious bludgeoning and Deeming's pulverised head fell limp. Lizzy couldn't move. Her buttocks were still poised and presented high in the air.

—THE MENARCHE! THE MENARCHE IS HERE! CRUCIFY THE MENARCHE!

The chorus of protest came from a group led by the eunuchs Gull and Sickert.

As well as being castrated for insubordination, both men appeared half devoured by syphilis. Their minds succumbed to insanity long before.

—CRUCIFY THE MENARCHE!

—KILL HER PLEBIAN SPIRIT!

The group of men grabbed Lizzy by the armpits and boarded her on a wooden crucifix. She could hear the 4th dimension, a better world—the sounds of the subway beneath her rattling through the curved sleepers of his ear canal. Lizzy closed her eyes and thought of the next world, the better world.

***

She woke up outside the city gates with that same

feeling of re-birth as before. She felt the sand beneath her knees, the great cross weighing heavy across her back. She tried to get up but kept toppling over.

Was this the 4th dimension?

Lizzy eventually made it to her feet and set off in the opposite direction from the clone metropolis, the second city of masturbating monsters.

She had trudged through the desert for almost thirty minutes before acknowledging the change in herself. Between her legs, something flapped against her inner thigh. Lizzy looked down and saw her latest affliction. In the distance a figure waved at her for help. The closer Lizzy got to the figure, more definable features emerged through the searing haze.

It was another woman. Lizzy's penis swelled and she was powerless once again . . .

HEART-ATTACK MAN

Hand clutched hard on chest
Terence, Mephisto & Viscera Eyes
Dreams of slaves at your behest
Terence, Mephisto & Viscera Eyes
Ambitions veil like a bleeding cataract
Terence, Mephisto & Viscera Eyes
To Cherry Island you'll set sail
Terence, Mephisto & Viscera Eyes . . .

Hearts explode, in time *you'll* see.

THE VERIDANT DREAM

ACKNOWLEDGMENTS

Thanks to Karen, Gordon, Casper, Jake and Lulu (the wild cat) for providing a nice countryside escape from the urban sprawl of it all. Thanks to Lauryn, Rachel, Darren, John, Joseph, Anne and Margaret for all the support and back-patting throughout the years.

High 5's to Seb Doubinsky, Michael Faun, Konstantine Paradias and Andrew Coulthard for all their professional encouragement, Christ knows I needed it!

Finally, thanks to Vincenzo for being a great friend, armchair psychiatrist and editor—and to Pat for accepting my second work of fiction for publication.

Miss you Louie.

ABOUT THE AUTHOR

Chris Kelso is a writer, editor and illustrator from Scotland. His books include include—*Schadenfreude* (Dog Horn Publishing), *Last Exit to Interzone* (Black Dharma Press), *A Message from the Slave State* (Western Legends Books), *Moosejaw Frontier* (Bizarro Pulp Press), *Transmatic* (MorbidbookS), *The Black Dog Eats the City* (Omnium Gatherum), *Terence, Mephisto & Viscera Eyes* (Bizarro Pulp Press) and *The Dissolving Zinc Theatre* (Villipede Publications). He also edited the anthologies *Caledonia Dreamin—Strange Fiction of Scottish Descent* (with Hal Duncan), *This is NOT an Anthology* and is the co-creator of *The Imperial Youth Review*.

All Art is Junk by R. A. Harris

Lana Rivers, a girl with paintbrush hair, is missing and it's up to Lancelot, her cyborg knight, and his bionic conjoined twin, Cilia, to find her before her evil father, a disrespected artist turned mad-scientist, performs a terrible experiment on her.

Cherub by David C. Hayes

Cherub wasn't like the other boys—too slow, too rough—but he didn't deserve what that hospital did to him, and now he will make them pay.

Skinners by Adam Millard

Los Angeles, the City of Angels. At least, that's what the brochure says. What it fails to mention is the earthquakes. Oh, and the flesh-eating creatures lying dormant beneath the concrete, waiting for the chance to surface once again. Their wait is over . . .

The After-Life Story of Pork Knuckles Malone
by MP Johnson

What's a farm boy to do when his pet pig becomes an evil, decaying hunk of ham with slime-spewing psychic powers?

A Lightbulb's Lament by Grant Wamack

A gentleman with a lightbulb for head wakes up in a world full of darkness, hooks up with a beautiful ex-prostitute, and an old man who can heal people; he travels down south to find the mysterious Creator.

The Horror Show by Vincenzo Bilof

A poetry novel—a narcoleptic, amnesiac Nobel Prize-winning poet becomes the subject of an experiment to cure madness.

Gravity Comics Massacre
by Vincenzo Bilof

An absolutely shitty novella involving comic books, aliens, a serial killer, teenagers in an abandoned town, horror-trope dream sequences, and an ending you're going to hate.

Glue by Scott Lange

Sticky bowels and sticky situations.

Ascent by Matthew Bialer

Is the 8 foot tall creature haunting a small town in Iowa in the fall of the year 1903 the product of a hoax and collective imagination or was it one of the first documented paranormal event in America? This epic poem grapples with these questions.

Fecal Terror by David Bernstein

A killer turd is on the loose!

Cucumber Punk by P. A. Douglas

Cucumbers, punks, and lumber. What's not to love?

Terence, Mephisto & Viscera Eyes
by Chris Kelso

9 new science fiction stories from Chris Kelso

Bizarro Bizarro: An Anthology

The finest bizarro short stories from 2013.

Captain K and the Bearded Man Boy by P. A. Douglas

Pat is a super hero and his alcoholic dog can talk. The world must surely be ending.

Day of the Milkman by S. T. Cartledge

In a world dominated by the milk industry, only one milkman survives after a terrible storm sinks all the ships and throws the Great White Sea out of balance.

Moosejaw Frontier by Chris Kelso

An unapologetic disaster of metafiction

Notes from the Guts of a Hippo by Grant Wamack

A rugged journalist travels to Brazil in search of a missing hippo researcher and the notes left behind lead to something earth shatteringly revelatory.

Industrial Carpet Drag by Bruce Taylor

Chemicals make you do great things!